Operation Death Watch

by

Leo Kessler

Dales Large Print Books
Long Preston, North Yorkshire,
BD23 4ND, England

British Library Cataloguing in Publication Data.

Kessler, Leo
    Operation death watch.

A catalogue record of this book is
available from the British Library

ISBN   978-1-84262-607-8 pbk.

First published in Great Britain 1985
by Century Publishing Co Ltd.

Copyright © Leo Kessler 1985

Cover illustration © Richard Clifton-Day by arrangement with
Alison Eldred

The moral right of the author has been asserted

Published in Large Print 2008 by arrangement with
Eskdale Publishing

Dales Large Print is an imprint of Library Magna Books Ltd.

Printed and bound in Great Britain by
T.J. (International) Ltd., Cornwall, PL28 8RW

'If ever there is a time when the utmost vigilance is required, it is upon this voyage.'

The Captain of the battleship
Prince of Wales, *August 1941*

AUTHOR'S PREFACE

I think there is a kind of second-hand nostalgia, which is even more poignant than the real thing. It is the sense of loss for places, people and events we only knew from yellowing newspapers, flickering black-and-white newsreels, the half-remembered radio broadcasts of those old days.

For me, that famous and daring voyage that the British Prime Minister Winston Churchill made across the U-boat infested Atlantic in that desperate summer of 1941 is touched with this artificial glow. It seems as vivid to me today as if I had personally been aboard that doomed ship, with the Old Man in his 'Teddy Suit' and all those others who were fated to die young and violently: 'Pay', 'Guns', Schoolie', 'Torps' and 'Toothie' and the rest of that strange closed society of the great battleship, men dead these forty years or more now...

In fact, on the spot there is little to be seen of that historic meeting between the two heads of state, which had occasioned the Great Man's daring unescorted voyage through U-boat filled waters to the other side of the world. Well might he declaim afterwards: 'Here was the only hope ... of saving the world from measureless degradation. And so we came back across the ocean waves, uplifted in spirit, fortified in resolve.' But what are the proofs, apart from those yellowing newspapers tucked away deep in the dusty stacks of public libraries, that Churchill ever met President Roosevelt in that lonely Canadian bay in the summer of 1941? What proof also is there that here the attempt was made to execute the most dastardly and far-reaching murder in the history of the 20th century?

The land around the bay is as lonely and barren of human habitation as it was then, nearly half a century ago. One half expects some savage Indian to appear from those dense fir forests or some buckskin-clad half-breed *trappeur* to come paddling his beechwood canoe down those still, cold creeks.

It is only when one approaches that ruined village, high on the cliffs above Placentia Bay, that one realizes that something *must* have happened that August in this remote place. Those charred timbers, half-buried in the undergrowth, were caused by the attacking Spitfires' incendiary bullets; and the ruined chimney-pieces, still standing among the wreckage, are pock-marked by the Canadian artillery shells. How else could those simple wooden crosses have come here, among the older weathered stone ones? And why do they bear no names?

Here, in what was once the hamlet of German Bay, its inhabitants long dead or fled, the great plot was hatched which was intended to force Britain to surrender to Nazi Germany and keep America out of World War Two. There is no doubt about it in my mind. The ruined village of German Bay and that great cave below, sealed these four decades or more, are the sole remaining testimony to World War Two's most devious and fiendish political assassination plan. Here it was that *THE WOLF PACK ATTACK* commenced...

Leo Kessler,
St John's, Newfoundland,
Winter 1985

PRELUDE

A Call to Action

'I hope we shall have an interesting and enjoyable voyage... And one not entirely without profit.'

Winston Churchill to his private secretary,
July 1941

With an angry snarl the Spitfire ripped across the bright wash of brilliant blue sky above London. All around it the flak peppered the air with puffs of grey smoke. The pilot did not notice. He was too intent on the kill now. Frantically the sinister black Heinkel fled across the rooftops of London, its port engine already trailing thick black smoke, braving the flak in a desperate attempt to escape the avenging fighter.

But there was going to be no escape for the 'Flying Pencil'. Second by second the fighter closed on its victim. At four hundred miles an hour, it streaked in for the kill, while below the two spectators stared upwards at it spellbound. Hastily the fat one dipped his big cigar in his whisky and took a quick grateful puff. Then it happened. There was a sudden harsh burst of fire. The Spitfire shuddered violently. Purple angry lights crackled the length of its wings. Like a myriad angry hornets, tracer zipped towards the Heinkel.

The bomber seemed to stop in mid-air. Black pieces of metal tumbled from it in a rain of death. For one long moment it hung in the sky, while the triumphant Spitfire hosed it with deadly fire. Startlingly, suddenly, it rolled on its back. A white puff of silk and a parachute blossomed below it. But only one. The next moment the Heinkel simply fell out of the sky. In a horrifying vertical dive, it shrieked down beyond the watchers' sight, while the victorious Spitfire pilot flung his plane into the victory roll before flattening out to streak away beyond the Thames to prepare for the next attack. Behind him he left a pyre of lazily ascending smoke and the first wail of the sirens from south London. It was the 'all clear'. The raiders had gone for the time being and the capital was free from attack again.

The Great Man beamed at his visitor, the tall, gaunt American, who in spite of the heat this hot July day was still wearing an ankle-length overcoat, which was as grey as his own lantern-jawed face. 'Well, my dear Harriman,' he growled in that well-known raspy voice of his, 'what finer introduction could you have to the spirit of Great Britain this summer of 1941 than that, eh?' He jerked his cigar at the bright blue sky. 'Britain fighting back!'

'Yessir, very fine, sir,' the American agreed as the Great Man took his arm as if they had known each other all their lives, and led him into the L-shaped garden of Number Ten, protected solely by a high brick wall. No detectives, no secret service agents, no police were in sight and Harriman told himself

18

solemnly this would not do for his boss. President Roosevelt never even left his office to go into the corridor in the White House without his full complement of security guards. In England, even in the middle of total war, security seemingly wasn't taken very seriously.

The Great Man paused and took another drink, followed by a puff on the enormous cigar before turning and beaming at his visitor from Washington. As always he had forgotten to put in his false teeth so that he looked to Harriman at this moment like some pink, toothless Buddha. 'Well, Harriman,' he commented as a barrage balloon which had broken away from its site floated over Number Ten like a fat grey slug, 'the British genius for survival has touched new heights, it seems. First Dunkirk, the Battle of Britain, a whole winter of blitzes, a whole ten months of them, with our great cities bleeding cruelly, and we,' he paused and looked directly at the American so that the latter shivered, telling himself he was looking at one of the world's greatest fighters, 'are still *here!* We've done it again somehow. Now at last we are no longer alone.'

'You mean the Russians, sir?'

'Yes, Harriman. After twelve months of going it alone, we have an ally and the Hun pressure is off a little.' The Great Man chuckled. 'I swear that I'd make a pact with the devil himself, as long as he would help me fight the Hun!'

Harriman allowed himself a polite chuckle, holding his claw of a hand in front of his mouth as he did so, as if he were afraid for some reason to reveal his teeth.

The Great Man's grin vanished and fire flashed from his blue eyes now. 'So we have made a start. But there is much to be done. It is not the beginning of the end, Harriman, not by a long chalk. I would say it is *the end of the beginning!* So,' he looked challengingly at the American, 'what news have you from the Former Naval Person, eh? Pray enlighten me.'

Harriman cleared his throat, as if he were preparing to give a long lecture. 'Mr Roosevelt, er the Former Naval Person, as you have code-named him, sir, is still fighting the Congress, as you know. The Isolationist lobby is strong. They are determined to keep America out of the war, just as the Former Naval Person is determined to take the States into the conflict on the side of Britain and Russia. But in this last week he has achieved the following. We are going to send troops to Iceland and protect the seaways off the island with the US Navy.'

The Great Man beamed. 'Excellent news, excellent, my dear Harriman! That will take a lot of pressure off our convoys from your country. And will the US Navy be prepared to sink German subs if they attack our convoys?'

Harriman nodded though his gaunt face looked suddenly worried. 'If American transports or merchant ships were involved, I am sure our ships would attempt to sink any German attacker. But sir, I do not think I am really that competent to tell the Presi – do forgive me – the Former Naval Person's most intimate thoughts on the future conduct of the war.' He sighed. 'It really is a pity that you can't meet him yourself, sir.'

From the south there came the first faint wail of the sirens. The *Luftwaffe* bombers were coming again. The Great Man did not seem to notice. Instead, in the sudden silence which had fallen over the walled garden, he puffed his cigar thoughtfully, moonlike face set as if he were thinking very hard.

Harriman waited. Now he could hear the first distant drum-roll of gunfire. The Germans were coming in force, he told himself. If only the President could be here now. In spite of the danger to his person, it would be the best means of showing him just what the British were like and how they were sticking it out under this merciless pounding by the enemy. 'The Former Naval Person really should know what is going on here, sir, from you personally.' He broke the silence. 'If the two of you could meet–'

He stopped suddenly. The other man had

raised his hand, face set and determined. 'I have not been made my sovereign's first minister to see this fine old country go down in defeat,' he growled defiantly in those familiar tones which had thrilled millions over the radio these last few terrible months. 'No sir! We *must* survive and we *will* survive. And I am prepared to undertake any kind of personal risk to ensure that we do. Do you think, Harriman,' he continued, voice back to normal now, as the bark and growl of the guns grew ever louder and the first black plumes of smoke from the bombs started to ascend into the bright blue summer sky, 'that the Former Naval Person would be prepared to meet Colonel Warden in some mutually convenient and neutral spot for a private conference? Tell me, pray.'

Harriman gasped, his sombre nature shaken by the bold suggestion. 'The press would get wind of it, sir,' he stuttered. 'There is no censorship in the States, sir. We would not be able to stop the newspaper hounds... We wouldn't be able to keep the meeting secret and there is no accounting for the reaction of the general public.'

The Great Man rumbled with suppressed laughter. 'That is exactly what we want them to know – *afterwards!* The great American public must become aware of this one single overwhelming fact. Namely this, that sooner or later the United States of America will have to go to war with the Japs and the Hun!' Suddenly he clutched Harriman's arm, as the first sinister black V of German dive-bombers appeared in the sky to the south-east. 'I shall call him, Harriman!' he exclaimed.

'Call who, sir?' Harriman asked, as the Spitfires roared into the attack yet once again. 'God,' he exclaimed to himself; he would never have imagined in his wildest dreams that besieged London was like this. The Krauts seemed to be attacking around the clock, but there was no doubt about it – the RAF was coping with the attacks exceedingly well. He would have to report that to the President when he got back to Washington.

'*The Former Naval Person,* of course, Harriman!' the Great Man chortled, highly pleased with himself and the way Fighter Command had stage-managed the Hun attacks, driving their bombers to the kill right in front of the American's eyes, as if they were beaters chasing grouse straight into the waiting guns. Harriman would undoubtedly report back to his chief just how efficient the RAF was, and how Britain could give it back to the Hun as well as take it.

'I shall invite him to a conference, the greatest conference of the war, Harriman, one which will – well – decide the fate of democracy and that of the Western World.'

Out of the corner of his eye the Great Man caught a glimpse of a flight of the sinister black dive-bombers breaking away from the main body. And they were heading in the direction of Number Ten!

He grabbed Harriman's arm urgently. 'Come, my dear fellow,' he cried above the snarl of racing engines. 'I think we have had our ration of luck for this day. *Let's make a run for it!*'

As the first Stuka flung itself out of the sky, its sirens howling eerily, filling the whole world with their fury, to commence its crazy ride of death, the two of them, the fat old man and the tall gaunt American, ran for their lives...

BOOK ONE

The Gathering of the Wolves

'My God, Doenitz, you can't mean it, can you? You suggest that we ... *that we assassinate Churchill!*'

Colonel-General Jodl to Admiral Doenitz,
July 1941

CHAPTER 1

'Stillgestanden!'

The harsh command echoed and re-echoed the length of the parade ground. Cawing and shrieking like lost babies the seagulls rose into the hard blue sky in protest. Three hundred pairs of jackboots stamped metallically onto the concrete. The long lines of blue-clad men, the tails of their flat caps fluttering in the wind that came from the estuary, stood rigidly to attention and waited.

Proudly, *Kapitänleutnant* von Arco, in charge of the parade, swung round, left hand clutching his ceremonial dirk, right hand touching his cap in naval fashion. 'U-Boat Flotillas One and Two – *all present and correct, Herr Admiral!*' he barked at the top of his voice, his weak, arrogant face, above the Knight's Cross at his throat, full of his own importance.

Admiral Doenitz, head of the German Submarine Service, acknowledged the salute, running his icy grey eyes along the ramrod-straight ranks of his crews, from the officers, no longer the bemedalled veterans of the early years, to the petty officers, most of them long-service men by the look of them, to the

27

ratings, eighty percent of them greenhorns straight from the training ships. He took his time, gazing at each face with that piercing, unwavering look of his, as if he were trying to imprint the features of each and every one of them on his mind's eye. Finally he was satisfied and barked, his thin cruel mouth working as if on steel springs, 'You may stand at ease!'

As one the sailors' right feet shot out and they placed their clasped hands behind their backs in the stand-at-ease position. They waited.

Again Doenitz took his time and in the front rank of the petty officers, all be-medalled veterans, big burly *Obermaat* Frenssen cracked an impatient, contemptuous fart and whispered out of the side of his mouth to his neighbour, 'Come on, Big Lion, they're giving away free suds and sauce on the *Lech* today.'

'Men of the Submarine Service... Comrades...!' Doenitz's harsh, rasping voice boomed from the loudspeakers, startling the gulls yet once again. 'I will not waste words, comrades. Soon you will sail to meet the English enemy once again. Our beloved Service has scored tremendous victories this year of 1941. Month after month we have sunk hundreds of thousands of tons of English shipping in the Atlantic. Slowly but surely we are draining the enemy of his life's blood. We

have had our losses, I know that, comrades. Kretschmar and Prien are no longer with us, like so many other of our heroes...'

Standing among the other executive officers, *Leutnant zur See* Christian Jungblut pursed his lips and felt a sudden sense of loss. This parade ground at Murwik was peopled with ghosts: the ghosts of those who had heard Doenitz's speech before and gone, never to return. This was his own fourth time. Would it be his last? He dismissed the thought hurriedly. Your nerve would soon go in the U-Boat Service, he told himself, if you started thinking like that. He concentrated on Doenitz's speech.

'But all of you, comrades, old hares and greenbeaks,' Doenitz was barking, 'will have to make one last effort. When the wolf packs of Flotilla One and Flotilla Two sail, each and every one of you must carry this conviction with you in your heart' Doenitz's hard flat face grew even harder and those icy grey eyes flashed a menacing fire – 'that every enemy ship you encounter must be destroyed ruthlessly and without compassion! This summer, comrades, we must destroy the might of perfidious Albion once and for all. *Kameraden der U-Boot Waffe*, long live our service! Long live our Germany! And long live our Führer Adolf Hitler! *Hoch ... hoch....!*

Three hundred husky young male voices took up the ringing cry and in their midst,

Christian, his handsome young face under his cropped blond hair flushed with sudden excitement, felt anew the thrill of battle, the heady sense of going out to fight to the death for one's country.

Obermaat Frenssen had other, less noble thoughts running through his mind at that precise moment, namely those of 'suds' and 'sauce', as he liked to call beer and schnapps. Hastily he stepped out of the ranks, ignoring von Arco's angry look. He wanted to bring the proceedings to a quick end and get on with the drinking. Once they sailed there'd be no more drink for weeks, perhaps even months to come. 'Three cheers for the Big Lion, comrades!' he bellowed at the top of his voice. 'Come on, you Lords, let's hear it. Hip, hip, *hurrah!*'

The parade ground burst in a tumult of cheers and Doenitz flushed with pleasure. Solemnly Frenssen winked at his neighbour. 'Now make way, matey, and let me belly up to that bar. This day I've got to take enough suds aboard to last till hell freezes over...!'

The wardroom of the *Lech*, the ancient steamer which served as a floating hotel for the officers and men of the Submarine Service when they were in Murwik, was loud with laughter, the clink of champagne glasses and the excited, brittle chatter of the men who might well soon be going to their deaths.

For already the two groups had separated, the 'base stallions', the elegant staff officers with their safe shore jobs, and the 'front swine', the men at the sharp end – the U-boat officers.

Christian Jungblut, bronzed and fit from his mountaineering leave in the South Tyrol, lounged at the fringe of the 'front swines' group, eyeing the 'base stallions' with a certain amount of cynical contempt. Of course, it was there that the mess stewards were busiest and most attentive. They didn't want a posting to sea-duty and the power lay there. All the women were there, too. The widows of the U-boat skippers already lost in the Battle of the Atlantic looking for a new husband and the security of a pension. And the new ones who knew that U-boat officers had a life expectancy of six months and were taking no chances. The 'base stallions' offered a better risk. Yes, there they were, flashing their teeth, making excited light conversation, full of girlish laughter, flirting outrageously with officers who could have been their fathers.

'A penny for them, *Herr Leutnant?*' a familiar voice broke into his cynical reverie.

Christian turned slowly, trying to resist the impulse to snap, 'Oh, go and piss in the wind!' as Frenssen would have done.

It was von Arco, of course, very elegant in his white summer uniform, with the

Knight's Cross dangling at his throat, face flushed a little with French champagne. If he had not been slightly drunk, Christian told himself, he would never have made this approach. Christian knew just what a coward von Arco was and how he had won that famous Knight's Cross of his.

'Oh, it's you, von Arco,' Christian said casually and took another sip of his champagne.

'You affect a very slack manner when addressing your superiors, Jungblut,' von Arco said, his arrogant face frowning suddenly.

Across the room, one of the war widows, whose husband's submarine had disappeared with all hands only two months before and who was looking very fetching in black silk, giggled tipsily and cried, 'Oh, what a flirt you are, Captain … I bet you turn all the girls' heads with your naughty remarks!'

Christian did not speak and von Arco snickered suddenly. 'You can have the lot of them if you're on the staff, you know, Jungblut. Most of them are no better than five-mark whores, pounding the pavement down in the *Reeperbahn*. Indeed, between you and me and the gatepost,' he covered his mouth with his elegantly manicured hand conspiratorially, 'I have had most of them myself. What do you say to that, eh?'

Christian let his pent-up resentment get the better of him. 'I see. But then, I never have had any dealings with whores. Will you excuse me? I think I'd like to move where the air is a little cleaner.'

Von Arco flushed crimson. 'Why you damned impudent–' he began, but Christian Jungblut had already vanished into the crowd of 'front swine'...

'I walked over tits, female tits, for four solid days first!' Frenssen exclaimed, face brick-red with drink, cap thrust to the back of his cropped head. 'Think of it, shipmates. Big luscious female knockers for seventy-two hours solid and never had a wink o' shut-eye. I said to the gash, have a good look at the floor, little cheetah, *cos yer gonna be on yer back, looking at the ceiling for the rest o' Frau Frenssen's handsome son's leave!*'

'The men of U-69 make love with their mouths!' someone sneered from close by in the crowded, smoke-filled bar. 'That's why they call it the sixty-nine. All muff-merchants, the lot of 'em!' The speaker sniggered and the rest of the barrel-chested old hares joined in.

Frenssen turned round slowly, clutching his beer mug in a fist like a small steam shovel. A coarse, brutalized face stared at him, a knowing look in the black eyes, a sneer set on the thick wet lips.

Frenssen took his time, while the rest of the petty officers waited for the explosion. 'Oh, it's you,' he said, 'Barthels of the U-23, the well-known Wanker from Wandsbek. Why, comrades, they tell he's just had an unfortunate love affair. *He broke his right hand! Ha ha....!*'

The others laughed uproariously at Frenssen's humour and Barthels flushed purple. 'Arse with ears!' he growled threateningly, deliberately pulling off his belt and wrapping it round his fist so that the metal buckle covered his knuckles.

Frenssen remained unmoved. 'Shove it, mate, or you'll lack a set o' ears in half a minute!' he growled and clenched his fist even more. 'I'd like nothing better to give you a knuckle sandwich, *piss-pansy!*'

'*Asparagus Tarzan!*' Barthels sneered, and added in a high-pitched falsetto that sounded like a girlish simper, 'Oh, you naughty sailor, you really frighten me ... I've creamed me skivvies already!' The others laughed. Frenssen raised his fist holding the beer mug. Barthels did the same with his belted one. The moment of confrontation had come. 'One more word,' Barthels breathed through gritted teeth, black eyes lethal, 'and you'll be spitting out yer biters all over the mess!'

'Shove it,' Frenssen hissed, '*shove it right up, shiteheel!*' He prepared to strike.

But that wasn't to be. Suddenly *Stabsobermaat* Maydag pushed his way in between the two enemies, wrinkled old face beneath his thatch of cropped grey hair serious and at

34

the same time sad. He was an old man for the Submarine Service – some said he had sailed with Doenitz when he had been a U-boat skipper himself in the Old War – but he did not hide behind his age like a lot of the base stallions. He still sailed on patrol into the Atlantic like the most junior petty officer. 'All right, you two rogues,' he barked, the authority of a quarter of a century in the *Kriegsmarine* behind him, 'that's enough of that. Drink your suds and sauce in peace. It's gonna be the last you're both gonna see for a long time.' He lowered his voice so that the others had to strain to hear his words. 'Perhaps for ever.'

The words sobered the two enemies up. They relaxed and Barthels started to unwind his belt from his fist, looking down at his big feet as if suddenly ashamed of himself.

Maydag made a great play of pulling out his battered old pipe and filling it with shag, while the others remained silent, their mood depressed by his last remark. Finally he was ready. Puffing on it, he looked around at the circle of faces and said, 'Never mind what the Big Lion says, comrades. He's allus had a big mouth. We're taking losses out there in the Atlantic, serious losses, and all you old hares, Frenssen, Barthels and the rest of you, know it. And the Tommy's fighting back. He's bottling up the U-boat arm in port after port, from Brest to Bergen. Why search the

Atlantic for us, he tells himself, when he can nab us as we leave port.' Slowly he pointed the stem of his old pipe at them almost accusingly. 'I'll tell yer this, comrades. Those of us who manage to get out into the North Sea without being attacked by the Tommies can count themsens frigging lucky, cos, don't you dare doubt, the Tommies will be out there – *now* – just waiting for some poor old submariner.' He fell silent and began to suck his old pipe morosely.

The good mood had vanished from the petty officers' last binge before they sailed. They sat slumped there hardly speaking, sipping their drinks sombrely, each man wrapped in a cocoon of his own thoughts, like men condemned to death...

CHAPTER 2

Little by little the dawn fog started to slip away. Now to the east the sun, still low on the horizon, started to flush the sky an ominous blood-red. As the U-69 steamed steadily westwards out of the estuary into the North Sea, their cover began to vanish and the lookouts now started to scan the sky anxiously. If the Tommies *were* waiting for them, it would be here.

The U-69's skipper, Captain Baer, whose appearance lived up to his name – he was bearded, burly and growled rather than spoke – spat angrily over the side of the conning tower. 'Shit weather, Number One,' he said in that throaty growl of his which seemed to come from the depth of his big seaboots. 'Why couldn't the damned fog have lasted until we were out in the North Sea?'

'Yessir,' Christian agreed dutifully, taking his gaze from the U-23 which had preceded them out of the estuary and which was now cutting through the waves at top speed, obviously well aware of the danger. 'And I don't suppose it would do much good to dive and proceed submerged?'

Baer tugged at his grizzled beard angrily.

'No, Number One, it wouldn't. The water's too shallow. Any half-blind Tommy pilot would be able to spot us at the depth. We've got to stick it out on the surface, by God. All right,' he dismissed the problem, 'keep a weather-eye skinned, Number One. I'm going below.'

Christian saluted and watched as the burly Captain squeezed himself down the tight hatch.

'Skinned like a peeled tomato,' Frenssen echoed, as the Skipper disappeared. 'The Tommies'll have to get up early to catch old Grizzly Bear out.'

'Have you no respect for your Captain, *Obermaat?*' Christian grinned at the use of the Captain's nickname. He certainly looked like a grizzly bear with all that shaggy hair. Idly he wondered what the crew of the U-69 called *him* behind his back; then he dismissed the thought and concentrated on the route ahead.

Now time passed leadenly. Anxiously the lookouts scanned the horizon as the crimson rays of the sun flushed the waves a bright red, heralding a beautiful early summer's day. But the lookouts had no time for the beauty of the morning. They knew just how precarious their situation was. They jumped every time a seagull came winging down, as if the damned marine scavengers were Tommy dive-bombers.

'Sir!' Frenssen said urgently. 'The U-23 is slowing down – *a lot!*'

Swiftly Christian flung up his glasses. The big petty officer was right. The U-boat was reducing speed radically; the froth of wild white water at her stern had vanished completely. 'What in three devils' name is their skipper up to, reducing speed *here?*' he exclaimed, puzzled and angry.

'Lot of piss-pansies on the U-23,' Frenssen growled, recalled Barthels, the 'Wanker of Wandsbek' and the rest of the other craft's petty officers, and spat contemptuously over the side.

Christian ignored him, his mind racing electrically. The skipper of the U-23 was an old hare; he knew the dangers of this particular strip of water. He wouldn't reduce speed unless it was absolutely necessary. Was he having engine trouble, perhaps? Hastily Christian adjusted his glasses even more finely and surveyed the other submarine. Now he could make out the dark figures lining both sides of her bows. There were more than the usual number of lookouts and they were holding long sticks, prodding the water with them. Suddenly Christian swallowed hard, as he realized what they were doing in the very same moment that Frenssen exclaimed: 'Shit on shingle! Now the clock is really in the bucket – *mines!*'

'*Mines!*' Christian exclaimed grimly. 'The

blasted Tommies have dropped mines over-night, after yesterday's sweep by our mine-sweepers. And you don't need a crystal ball to know why.'

'Yer,' Frenssen agreed miserably, eyes already beginning to flash over the surface of the water looking for those lethal black horns. 'The shitehawks want to pin us down here at slow speed until their Sunderlands can come along and drop a nasty square egg on us!'

'Exactly.' Hastily Christian bellowed down the tube, 'Executive to Captain. Mines, sir!'

'By the Great Whore of Buxtehude where the dogs bark with their tails,' Captain Baer growled, *'now this!* What a shitting life. All right, I'm come up topside.'

Half a minute later the U-69 had reduced speed to a snail's pace and to port the first deadly black ball, containing half a ton of high explosive appeared, bobbing up and down silently, waiting, waiting, waiting…

Now the U-23 and the U-69, separated by a few hundred metres only, crawled across the blood-red sea. All was tense, nerve-racking expectancy. Guns were manned, double lookouts posted, and the decks of both sub-marines were lined with anxious ratings, armed with boat-hooks ready to ward off any mine that came too close. And they were everywhere. As Captain Baer had snarled,

'My God, the Tommies must have used all their air force to drop this lot! The bastards are everywhere!'

'Let's hope they did, sir,' a worried Christian had replied, 'and that their crews are safely tucked away in their sacks after a big egg-and-bacon breakfast, because if their pilots catch us out here at this speed...' He had not completed the rest of his sentence. He had not needed to. Baer knew, just like the rest of the crew, exactly what their fate would be in that case.

Now the U-23 to their front had almost stopped moving. Across the intervening space, the tense crew of the U-69 could hear the curses of the other crew as they edged their way, inch by inch, by a mine which had just scraped the U-23's bow. Sweating, pale-faced ratings hung onto the mine grimly, their boat-hooks carefully inserted between the mine's horns as they walked along the craft.

'Holy strawsack!' Frenssen cursed, as he squatted behind the conning tower machine-gun, gaze constantly sweeping the sky for the first sight of an enemy plane. 'I even feel sorry for the "Wanker of Wandsbek".'

A minute later they had their own mine. There was that ominous grating on their hull in the very same instant that a frightened lookout cried, 'Mine to starboard!'

Christian felt his heart miss a beat. Next

to him, Captain Baer bellowed urgently, *'Stop both … quick!'*

Christian swung himself onto the ladder and pelted down to the deck as the U-69 came to a dead stop. Up ahead, on the starboard bow, two ashen-faced ratings were exerting all their strength, their muscles rippling through their thin singlets, as they attempted to push the half-ton mine away from the hull. Christian raced up to them. He grabbed a boat-hook from a bemused third rating, his eyes wild and wide with unreasoning fear, and thrust it too against the dripping black monster.

'Heave, men … come on, put yer backs into it,' he gasped, as leaning forward, as if poling a punt, he exerted all his strength. *'Heave!'*

On the conning tower, Captain Baer acted now that he saw the three of them had succeeded in pushing the mine a little way from the hull, though he knew that the slightest wave could wash the deadly metal ball right back up against the hull. 'Both ahead,' he whispered into the tube, as if he dared not speak in his normal gruff bass. 'Slow … dead slow!' Then he closed his eyes for an instant, as if saying a silent prayer to himself that they might escape the mine.

Slowly, terribly slowly, the U-69 inched its way forward, the two ratings and Christian locked to the mine, easing it along the side

its outer fringes and while the U-boats plodded on at their snail's pace, they'd attack from both flanks. They, the U-boats, were flies which had clumsily flown into the spider's web where, trapped as they were, they would be consumed at the spider's leisure. 'Damn it!' he cursed aloud with rage. 'That's not going to be!'

He swung round at the sweating, panting gunners, crouched behind the shield, whirling their wheels, thrusting home a shell into the gaping maws of the breech, frantically trying to keep the whirling, swerving attackers in their sights. 'Concentrate on that one on the right flank, petty officer!' he snapped at the *Obermaat* in charge. 'By the amount of bunting and aerials he's carrying, he could be the flotilla leader. Knock him out and we could delay them a bit.'

'Yessir,' the petty officer barked, not taking his gaze off the enemy for one minute.

Christian doubled along the deck and hastily swung himself up the conning tower. Already the U-23 had commenced firing and the metallic boom of their gun echoed across the water. He dropped over the side, while Baer watched the U-23's frantic efforts to straddle one of the tremendously fast British craft with their shells. 'You know what they've done, sir,' he cried without ceremony.

Baer groaned miserably as the U-23's gunners missed yet once again. 'Yes,' the Captain yelled above the sudden throaty bark of their own gun, 'they've caught us with our drawers well and truly around our ankles!'

'Not that, sir,' Christian cried desperately, ducking instinctively as a burst of enemy machine-gun fire ripped the length of the conning tower. 'They've got us pinned down in this minefield; and they know the extent of it so they can move with impunity. So, sir, it's all a question of reaching roughly where they are now – perhaps some two sea miles or more. Then we can move freely, submerge, the lot.'

'Agreed, Number One,' Baer yelled as behind them a furiously cursing Frenssen let rip a tremendous burst of machine-gun fire. 'The only problem is, *we've got to reach that shitting area first!*'

'Dive, sir!' Christian screamed as the leading MTB heeled suddenly and something grey and deadly slid into the water in an abrupt flurry of white bubbles. *'Dive, sir... It's our only chance... DIVE....!'*

CHAPTER 3

Kapitänleutnant von Arco, his arrogant weak face set hard and intent as he bent over the cipher clerk's shoulder, waited impatiently. Next to him the English-speaking signals officer listened in by means of the attachment, hardly daring to breathe in case he missed something. The naval engineers and scientists had done a tremendous job. They had never pulled off a feat like this before in nearly three years of war.

Von Arco swallowed and tried to forget the slim nubile body of Frau von Prittwitz, widow of the celebrated skipper of U-88, who had once been his classmate at the Academy. It was easy to tell that she had not had a man for a long time. Klaus von Prittwitz, now resting and rotting away somewhere at the bottom of the Atlantic Ocean, had probably never realized just what a little treasure had been his, he told himself. Why, she had known more delightful little tricks than those highly-priced French whores he had patronised in Paris the previous year. It had been an absolute ecstatic delight, the slow, tantalizing way she had bent and taken his–

'Sir,' the excited signals lieutenant broke into his reverie of last night's sexual conquest, 'it is him!'

'*Who?*' von Arco demanded.

'The big one!' the other officer gasped. '*President Roosevelt!* There's no mistaking that voice anywhere. I remember it well from when I was in the States before the war. Every so often he'd give a fireside chat, as they called–'

'Piss in the wind with your fireside chats, whatever they may be, Lieutenant!' von Arco snorted angrily. 'You are sure it is that Jew Roosevelt?'

'Absolutely, sir,' the Lieutenant said, eyes wild with excitement, cheeks flushed.

'Who's he talking to?' von Arco demanded, as the cipher clerk started to scribble rapidly on his pad. The signals officer flung up his hand for silence and von Arco broke off abruptly as the cipher clerk pressed the earphones as if he were having difficulty in hearing.

Von Arco waited tensely once more. Ever since the beginning of the war the German *Kriegsmarine* had been tapping the transatlantic cable between London and New York, but never before had the navy's engineers been able to listen in to a scrambled telephone call through it. Now they had finally succeeded and it appeared they were going to have a real breakthrough: a mess-

48

age of world-shattering importance.

Outside on the barracks square a bunch of new recruits to the *Kriegsmarine* were hopping across the wet concrete, arms extended like some sort of blue-suited penguins, while the coarse-voiced instructor barked, '*Los* ... *los*... *Tempo*... *Tempo*... Open yer legs, willya, you bunch o' wet-tails. Nothing'll fall out of 'em! Move it you piss-pansies... *LOS!*'

'A Colonel Warden, *Herr Kapitänleutnant*,' the signals officer hissed. 'Roosevelt is talking to some colonel named Warden.' Suddenly he looked puzzled. 'But what would a President be doing talking to a lowly colonel over the transatlantic telephone, sir? I don't quite understand.' He faltered, gazing in bewilderment at the sudden look of triumph crossing the senior officer's face. 'Do you, sir?'

'Don't ask any more damned questions!' von Arco barked. 'Get on with your job. What are Roosevelt and this, er' – he caught himself just in time – '*Colonel Warden* talking about? Hurry – translate!'

'Yessir ... immediately, sir,' the signals officer snapped.

Outside, the recruits were being chased back and forth, crimson-faced and gasping for breath. Every five metres or so their instructor would order them to drop full-length to the ground, just where there was a particularly deep puddle. Most of them were soaked already and many of them were staggering about like chronic alcoholics. Von Arco noted their condition with disgust. He told himself that recruits to the German Submarine Service were getting softer by the month. Discipline would have to be tightened up even more. That rabble down there was not at all the type an elite service demanded. He must mention the matter to the Big Lion.

Now the signals officer began to translate the conversation taking place over three thousand miles away into hesitant German: *'Will meet in the Atlantic...* This Colonel Warden, he will *cross in the greatest secrecy,* they say...'

Von Arco's brain raced madly. He felt an electric tension surge through his blood as he started to consider the exciting possibilities that this phone tap opened up. My God, it might even mean the end of the war, he told himself. Perhaps this was the most important event in his whole career.

'Roosevelt says he will try to keep his departure as secret as he possibly can, sir... He will sail in his yacht the 'Potomac'... The American press will be told that he is taking his annual summer cruise off New England... It will be put out it is quite a routine thing...'

Von Arco swallowed hard, trying to repress his rising excitement. All the pieces were falling into place. Now they even knew roughly where the two of them, 'Colonel Warden' and the 'Former Naval Person' would meet. It would be the area – say – between Iceland, Canada and the New England seaboard. Admittedly it was very large, but if they could concentrate every available U-boat...

He broke off his reverie. The signals officer had held up his hand, his young face strained and tense. 'We've got a date, *Herr Kapitän-leutnant,*' he announced, cocking his head to one side as if he were having difficulty in hearing.

'Yes,' von Arco urged hurriedly. 'Spit it out, man!'

'This Colonel Warden is suggesting he will sail on ... August fourth ... on the battleship the *Prince of Wales* ... and Roosevelt is agreeing.'

'And the date they will meet?'

'Roosevelt isn't sure, sir.' The signals officer strained hard, while von Arco felt a nerve ticking excitedly at the side of his face. The stress was almost unbearable now. What a tremendous coup this really was! 'You see, sir, Roosevelt says it's a question of cruising speeds and such matters.' The signals officer let his shoulders slump with relief suddenly. At the desk the cipher rating sat back and wiped the glistening beads of sweat from his forehead, easing off the earphones gradually. The conversation was over.

For a moment there was absolute silence

in the tight, airless room, broken only by the muted cries of the recruits outside. They were dropping now into the sand pit from a ten metre-high tower, urged on by the contemptuous cries of the instructor. One of them had dropped unluckily and was writhing in pain at the side of the pit. Von Arco noted with approval that the petty officer was paying no attention to him. Recruits to the submarine service had to be as hard as Krupp steel. There was no place in the *Kriegsmarine's* elite for weaklings.

At the desk the cipher clerk finished scribbling down his transcript of the intercepted message, which he now handed to the signals officer for checking and counter-signing. The latter did so swiftly. Hastily he added his initials and passed it on to von Arco. 'Sir,' he said hesitantly, for at the Submarine Service's HQ at Murwik, it was well known just what an arrogant dog *Kapitän-leutnant* von Arco was, 'can I ask you something.'

Von Arco looked at him haughtily, as if he were seeing him for the first time. 'You can, though whether you will receive an answer or not, this is entirely another matter.'

The signals officer flushed, but persisted. 'But who is this – er – Colonel Warden, sir? Is he important?'

Von Arco smiled coldly. He told himself it might be opportune to let the young fool into the great secret. Later when it was all over, he would undoubtedly blab and let the whole HQ know it was *Kapitänleutnant* von Arco who had hatched the whole world-shaking plot. 'Buzzes' always ran riot at Murwik. By God and All His Triangles, if this thing worked, he would end the war an admiral yet! He crooked a finger at the signals officer. 'Come over here, lieutenant,' he said and steered him away from the cipher clerk.

Together they crossed over to the window. Down below, the recruit still writhed in the sand, unattended to as yet, a thin trickle of blood escaping from his left leg which was twisted at a strange angle. Automatically von Arco told himself the fellow would be finished now in the Submarine Service. He'd probably end up on the newly opened Russian front, dying for Folk, Fatherland and Führer in some God forsaken Popov field. He dismissed the man and said: 'I must warn you, Lieutenant, that this matter is now highly secret. Reveal one word of what I am going to say to you now and you will be in serious trouble, very serious trouble. Got it?'

'Got it, sir,' the other officer replied eagerly, eyes shining.

'Well then, Lieutenant, for your private information this is who your Colonel Warden is.' Von Arco's eyes bored into the other man's innocent, clean-cut face. 'He is no other than that drunken sot who controls the destinies of the English people in London. He is – *Winston Churchill!*'

The signals officer could not quite stifle his gasp of surprise. *'Grosser Gott!'* he exclaimed. 'Do you mean, sir, that Roosevelt and Churchill are going to meet somewhere in the North Atlantic soon?'

'I do,' von Arco replied, his arrogant face revealing none of the burning excitement within him. 'And I have a certain feeling that the Big Lion will be sending his – hm – own personal representative to attend that particular meeting, too.' He laughed abruptly but there was no warmth in the laugh and the young signals officer felt an icy finger of fear trace its way down the small of his back. He shivered. 'You mean, sir–' he began, but von Arco stopped his comment with an imperious gesture. 'I mean nothing,' he snapped harshly and with that *Kapitänleutnant* von Arco was gone, leaving the young officer staring blankly at the wall in front of him, mind racing as he wondered what the arrogant bastard was intending to do with his tremendous new secret...

CHAPTER 4

As the klaxons shrieked and anxious petty officers bellowed orders, there came that dreaded boom of metal striking metal. *'They've hit the U-23!'* Christian Jungblut yelled urgently, as the compressed air hissed from the U-69's tanks and she prepared to dive. 'Torpedo midships! She's sinking–'

His cry was interrupted by another tremendous boom. The U-23 seemed to rise for a moment and later Christian would swear he had seen her screws churning purposelessly in the air. Here and there panicked sailors threw themselves overboard. But the rest had no time to. Suddenly a great scorching blowtorch shot the length of the stricken submarine, burning away everything in its path.

Christian gasped in horror as a sailor, already aflame, tried to escape that dreadful fire. To no avail. It swallowed him in its greedy fire-red maws. He disappeared, transformed in an instant into a shrunken, charred pygmy.

'Come on, Jungblut!' Baer cried desperately from below. 'We're diving, man. *Los!*'

Christian flung one last glance at the dying

U-23, now completely submerged in flame, what was left of her crew huddled undoubtedly below, waiting for death to come for them, then he was skidding down the dripping iron ladder into the control tower. A moment later he had flung the hatch to and was standing there in the green-glowing light, dripping with seawater and ashen-faced, eyes wide and wild with what he had just seen.

'Lieutenant,' a voice called.

He turned slowly and stiffly like an automaton.

It was Frenssen, big tough face full of concern. 'Here you are, sir,' he hissed. 'Take a slug of this.'

Hardly aware of what he was doing, Christian accepted the little bottle which Frenssen had palmed to him. It was Frenssen's illegal 'flatman', filled with contraband booze. But at this moment he was not concerned with regulations. He needed a drink – badly. He took a stiff pull at the little flat bottle and shuddered as the fiery liquid slammed into the back of his throat. 'Thanks, Frenssen … thanks a lot,' he whispered, shaking his head like a man trying to wake up from a heavy sleep.

'Allus keep one handy, sir,' Frenssen answered with a wink. 'Strictly for medicinal purpose of course.'

'Of course,' Christian allowed himself a faint grin, then he crossed to where the

Captain stood.

Baer looked worried, but confident. 'My guess, Jungblut,' he said without any preliminaries, 'is that we are on the very edge of the minefield. Now if we can make those couple of hundred metres still left safely, we've done it. The damned Tommy MTBs don't have depth charges or Asdic listening devices, as far as I know. So they present no danger.'

'Agreed, sir. The only thing they can do, sir, is to whistle up the RAF.'

'Exactly, but unless we're very unlucky, we might well have darkness by then and we can run on the surface. With our diesels we can put a lot of sea miles between us and this cursed place. Then–' He broke off abruptly.

There was no mistaking that metallic scraping noise on the hull outside. They had knocked into a mine. For one long moment no one spoke, no one moved. In that eerie green-glowing light they remained rooted to the spot, transfixed, eyes big and staring with horror. The scraping continued.

In a hoarse whisper, Captain Baer ordered, 'Both engines – slow, dead slow!'

Behind Christian, who could feel the cold sweat beginning to trickle down the small of his back, someone started to pray fervently.

Still that dreaded sound of metal rubbing against metal continued. Christian felt himself clenching his fists, his heart thumping madly, as if it might burst his breast-cage at any moment. You did not need to have much imagination, he told himself, to know that at this very moment all their lives hung on a very frail thread. The slightest pressure against one of those horns that protruded everywhere from the deadly metal ball and it would go up, taking them with it.

Next to Captain Baer, Frenssen started to count off the seconds, estimating mentally how long it would take the mine at this speed to run the length of the hull. *'Four ... five ... six...'* He jumped visibly and his voice almost broke as the U-boat gave a sudden lurch. Nothing happened and he wiped the sweat from his contorted face with a hand that shook visibly. *'Seven ... eight ... nine.'*

The scraping stopped abruptly and Frenssen, unable to stand the tension any longer, cried with heartfelt relief, *'TEN... FRIGGIN' TEN... WE'VE FRIGGING WELL DONE IT, SHIPMATES!'* He sat down suddenly, shoulders bowed, all energy drained out of him, as if someone had opened an invisible tap.

'Phew!' Captain Baer leaned against the bulkhead weakly and grinned at Christian. 'Ten, frigging ten it is, Number One.' He sighed again and then new hope and energy began to surge into his blood. He raised his voice, now crisp and businesslike again. 'All right, engineer, both ahead ... full speed...

Move it now!'

The soft purr grew in intensity. The U-69 surged forward through a free sea at last. She was on her way to join the wolves once more...

Four hours later the U-69 surfaced once more. It was not yet dark, but a grey gloom spreading in across the dark heaving sea from the east heralded the end of that long terrible day.

The MTBs had passed. So had what had survived of their wolf pack. But there were signs enough of their passing. The waves were black with ship's oil and flotsam, bobbing up and down sluggishly.

Baer lowered his glasses. 'One of the Thorn Wolf Pack,' he said slowly and without animation, for the scene was far too sombre for excitement, 'must have sunk a Tommy. Look over there.' Christian followed the direction of his gaze. A long black rubber dinghy was moving across the surface of the limitless sea. In it there was a man. But even without his glasses, Christian could see he was dead. He squatted there too stiffly, his teeth a gleaming white against the black oil mask of his face. They passed each other and Christian forced himself to look at this pitiful relic of the sea, black, stone-cold already, jogged back and forth by the motion of the waves, purposeless and somehow disgusting in death. He shivered and was glad when the lone dinghy with its cargo of death floated away.

But if Christian was nauseated by the dead Englishman, there were others happily engaged in retrieving what they could from the waves, eagerly fishing for bottles and crates. The old hares knew that the English ships were well supplied. With a bit of luck they might fish out a carton of Woodbines or, even better, the prized Lucky Strikes; or if they were extra lucky an illicit bottle of Navy rum, which would be stowed away hurriedly before one of the deck officers saw it. Led by *Obermaat* Frenssen – naturally – they scampered back and forth along the slippery deck, trying to grab the floating crates with those self-same boat-hooks with which they had fought to ward off the killer mines only hours before in what seemed now another age.

Christian shook his head in mock wonder. 'Just look at them, sir. Like schoolkids just let out of school. You wouldn't think that today they had nearly been finished for good!'

Baer tugged his grizzled beard and nodded sagely. 'Perhaps it is better that way, Number One. If you start to think about the things that happen to you on active service in the Submarine Service it isn't long before the fellers in the white coats come to take you away to the funny farm in their rubber vans. Yessir!'

Christian laughed at Baer's choice of words and said, 'Suppose you're right, sir.' He raised his voice. 'Have we our orders yet, sir?'

'Yes, I opened the sealed orders just before I came up onto the bridge. Wolf Pack Thorn is to operate in the general area of Southern Iceland, Canada and American Eastern Seaboard. Captain Thorn will radio additional orders once we have details of the sailings of Allied convoys. All very routine.'

'Yessir, all very routine,' Christian agreed, but at the back of his mind a hard, cynical little voice sneered, *'Routine?* Yes, if you consider slaughtering scores of your fellow human beings, who you have never met before and with whom you have no quarrel, routine.' Christian dismissed the voice, and scrutinized their front. Ahead the Aurora Borealis flickered, its streamers twisting like cold flames, changing colour all the time, growing and fading, casting an eerie, unearthly glow over the U-69, alone in this grey northern sea. Involuntarily Christian shuddered as he considered that one of those glowing figures might suddenly press down and force the submarine to the bottomless depths.

'What's the matter, Number One,' Baer snapped. 'Louse ran over yer liver?'

'Something like that, sir. I was just thinking how big this all is and how small and insignificant we are.'

Baer hesitated for a moment, staring at the strange flickering fire in the heavens, too. 'Anyone with half a soul in him always does the same, Number One. You aren't the only one, you know. But repress that imagination. Remember the gents in the white coats and the rubber vans to take you to the funny farm.'

'The funny farm it is, sir.'

'All right, I'm going below. Watch those rogues down there don't fall in the water. It's going to be a long patrol. We'll need the lot of them.'

'Yessir.'

Captain Baer pulled hard at his battered white hat – only the skipper was allowed to wear a white naval cap – and clattered down the ladder, leaving Christian alone, staring at those eerie flickering lights and wondering to himself.

Down below Frenssen chortled hugely and tucked a second bottle of illicit British rum inside his leather jacket. 'Holy strawsack, mates,' he cried with delight, 'this patrol is like frigging Christmas! Two bottles of sauce already and we ain't started yet. Christmas all the frigging way…' But for once *Obermaat* Frenssen was going to be wrong, very wrong.

CHAPTER 5

'*Meine Herren,*' the blond giant bellowed at the top of his voice, as the huge ornate doors of the Reich Chancellory started to swing open ceremoniously, '*unser Führer – Adolf Hitler!*'

As one the brilliant assembly of senior officers from all three armed services, most of them with the purple stripe of the Greater German High Command down the side of their trousers, and ministers in frock coats and striped pants, snapped to attention and raised their right hands in salute.

Almost casually Hitler, the new master of a Europe which stretched from the Channel to the Vistula and from the Arctic Circle to the Mediterranean, threw back the lock of black hair hanging over his forehead and flipped back his own hand to acknowledge the salute. For a long moment he paused there and surveyed the crowd of officers and officials waiting to see him. Some of them, he knew, would wait for days for the chance of five minutes' conversation with him. It was a heady feeling and reminded him again of just how much might he exercised this victorious summer of 1941. Why, he was the most powerful man on earth! His dark eyes swept along their eager faces, deciding who he would see this morning before contemptuously dismissing the rest to wait for another day. Behind him his new secretary Martin Bormann, fat and stocky, looking with his pugnacious chin like a boxer who had run to seed, waited with his notebook poised.

Suddenly Hitler's gaze came to rest on a hard, inflexible face, dominated by two pale-grey eyes. It was Doenitz, the Head of the Submarine Service.

Hitler's face softened and he broke into a warm smile. This summer Doenitz's U-boats had presented him with nearly a million tons of sunken British ships; if anyone could bring the obstinate English to their knees so that they would finally see sense and make peace, it would be Doenitz. He moved forward, hands extended in welcome. Immediately the elegant crowd parted to left and right in order to let Hitler through. Behind him Bormann noted, with that usual malicious sneer of his on his broad face, that there were looks of envy and hate on all sides. Doenitz was obviously not a popular man in the Reich Chancellory.

Doenitz and, at his side, von Arco clicked to attention as Hitler swept towards them. They flung up their right hands and cried in unison: 'Heil Hitler!'

'My dear Admiral,' Hitler cried, seeming not to hear the greeting, 'how good it is to see you here.' He took Doenitz's hand and began to shake it warmly while von Arco looked on, glowing with pride. Already fat Professor Hoffmann, Hitler's personal photographer, was sneaking up to take a picture of the meeting. Undoubtedly his photograph would be on the front pages of every newspaper in the Reich tomorrow morning. Soon the whole of the *Kriegsmarine* would know that *Kapitänleutnant* von Arco was a coming man: someone to be reckoned with. Arrogant and high-handed as he was, von Arco could never bear not to be the centre of attention; and at this very moment he and his Chief were exactly that, as the others stared at the little scene with a mixture of envy and hatred.

'Mein Führer,' Doenitz barked, his contempt for the hangers-on and courtiers all too obvious, 'may I have permission to talk to you immediately – *and alone?'*

Even the Führer looked a little surprised, and behind him Bormann whistled softly through his dingy teeth. It took a bold man, or one who had some vital plan, to talk to Adolf Hitler like that. 'Where's the fire, Doenitz?' Hitler tried to joke. 'Is what you wish to say to me *that* important?'

Doenitz was completely devoid of humour. He rasped immediately, 'It is, *mein Führer,* and it is something that can only be explained without the presence of others. I think, sir, you will agree when you have heard what I have to relate.'

For a moment Hitler hesitated. Then he made up his mind, impressed by the sailor's boldness and the hard, certain look in those icy eyes. 'All right then, Doenitz, you will have your way. I take it you do not object to Jodl and Keitel being present?' He indicated his two military advisers, pale-faced, cunning Colonel-General Jodl and the ramrod-straight, wooden Field Marshal Keitel. Hitler gave a little smile.

But again humour was wasted on Doenitz. 'No sir, I would not object to just the two of them.'

'Na schön,' Hitler conceded. 'All right, Bormann, see to it that we are not disturbed. We shall go into the map room.' And with that the little group, ushered out by the giant black-clad SS adjutants, vanished behind the great doors, leaving behind them that elegant crowd seething with angry rumours and recriminations...

Hitler snapped his fingers as they took their places around a great map of the Atlantic which von Arco had unfolded on the big table in front of them. 'Well, Doenitz, what is it?'

'Mein Führer, Churchill is sailing for

America in August.'

Hitler blanched. *'What did you say?'*

'Sir, he is to sail for America secretly and meet Roosevelt somewhere off the American coast,' Doenitz snapped, then paused. He had caught Hitler's interest, he knew. Now he could wait until asked to explain his plan.

'So the Jewish plutocrat and the sottish lackey meet at last, eh,' Hitler mused. His voice rose, suddenly filled with anger. 'No doubt the two of them, egged on by the Yiddish press and power circles in both their countries, will be hatching plans for fresh mischief against the Reich.' Hitler rolled his dark eyes in despair. 'What have we done to earn their hatred, *meine Herren?* Have we not tried to save Churchill's face ever since we ran the English out of Europe at Dunkirk last year? Have we not offered him complete freedom to run the affairs of the British Empire in peace as long as he leaves continental Europe to us? Doesn't the fat fool realize that if he continues this war he will lose his precious empire to the colonials...'

Doenitz listened expressionlessly while Hitler ranted on, his mind full of his plan. But von Arco was impressed, as were all those who met Hitler for the first time. What genius Hitler showed, he told himself, immensely flattered to be thus in the Führer's presence.

Finally Hitler ran out of steam, as Doenitz knew he would, and he stepped in immediately, repeating his initial statement for Hitler's benefit: 'So Herr Churchill is going to cross the Atlantic. Important politically no doubt, but what concern is it to the *Kriegsmarine* and, in particular, to the Submarine Service?' He answered his own question quickly before Hitler could butt in. '*This!* Politically we all know Churchill's aim. He wants to drag the Americans into the war in order to rescue his miserable little island from the mess it is in. Sooner or later Churchill will succeed in this aim, especially now that the Russians are involved in the war. Now' – suddenly Doenitz slammed his pale white fist down on the table so that even the Führer started – 'is the time to stop him before he achieves that aim of dragging the *Amis* into the war!'

'*Stop him?*' Hitler echoed in bewilderment.

Doenitz flashed a quick look at von Arco who had first suggested the great plan. '*Jawohl, mein Führer*,' he rasped dourly. 'If Herr Churchill never reaches America there will be *no* coalition between America and England. There is nobody in that country who can take his place.'

Hitler stepped back a pace, as if an invisible hand had slammed into his chest, suddenly very pale. Next to him, Jodl gasped, 'My God, Doenitz, you can't mean it, can you? You suggest that we … *that we assassinate Churchill?*'

Doenitz nodded solemnly, his face revealing nothing. 'Yes,' he answered simply, looking at the shocked General, 'I do.'

'But my dear Admiral,' Jodl objected, 'a sovereign state simply does not do things like that. Assassinate the head of another country, even if that state is an enemy one? My God, Doenitz, what are you thinking of?'

Doenitz could barely conceal his contempt. *'Herr Generaloberst,'* he snapped through gritted teeth, 'this is the age of total war and total war demands total solutions – those of the twentieth century. We are no longer gallant, chivalrous soldiers fighting some comic 19th century war. In this year of 1941 we are fighting for our very existence and every method has to be used in order to win that fight.' His cold eyes flashed fire. 'Why batter for years at the body, when with one swift stroke you can sever the head and fell the monster immediately?'

'How right you are, Doenitz!' Hitler cried enthusiastically, suddenly transformed. 'With Churchill – er – eliminated, the English will cave in. Chamberlain, that old fool, might be dead,' his face contorted in disgust, 'but there are many other Chamberlains over there in London who will be only too eager to sue for peace with the Reich–' Hitler hesitated suddenly. 'But my dear Doenitz,' he continued, 'how will it be done?'

Doenitz looked at von Arco. *'Kapitänleutnant von Arco,'* he barked, as if he were on the barracks square back at his headquarters in Murwik, *'zum Vortrag bitte.'*

Proudly von Arco drew himself up to his full height, arrogant face flushed and pointed at the huge map. *'Mein Führer,* Herr Churchill has picked the Royal Navy's fastest, newest and probably most powerful ship to cross the Atlantic to meet Herr Roosevelt, the *Prince of Wales.* It is hardly likely that any German surface or underwater craft would be able to intercept her, even if we knew her route across, which we don't.'

Hitler nodded. 'Yes, I know of the ship. It was one of those which helped to sink our *Bismarck* recently. A ship like that deserves to be sunk. But no matter, pray continue, *Herr Kapitänleutnant.'*

'Thank you, *mein Führer.* So there is little we can do while the *Prince of Wales* crosses the Atlantic, but there is a great deal we can do *when she has reached the other side!'*

Hitler's eyes narrowed. 'How do you mean?'

'I mean this, sir,' von Arco replied hastily. 'Once she has completed the dash across the Atlantic, she will undoubtedly refuel at either a Canadian or Newfoundland port and then commence her journey to the place of rendezvous with the President's yacht, the *Potomac*. Now we are working on the assumption that our agents in America and especially in the American media, the press and radio, will be able to inform us eventually of the President's ship's movements. So we–'

'–Can use the *Potomac's* movements to lead us to the *Prince of Wales!*' Hitler burst in excitedly. '*Grossartig...! absolut genial!*' he exclaimed, sallow face flushed with joy at the thought of what was going to happen to his old enemy. 'We could sink the *Prince of Wales* and Churchill in front of the President's very eyes. *Himmel, Herr Gott!* That would demonstrate the power of the Third Reich and show the Jew Roosevelt that *nothing* and *no one* can escape the long arm of the New Order!'

While Hitler talked on, seized by a wild, almost crazed excitement, von Arco flashed a quick look of enquiry at Doenitz. The latter nodded his head gently. The sinking of the *Prince of Wales* in front of Roosevelt's eyes had not been part of their original plan. But Doenitz knew it was unwise to quibble with the Führer about small things. Naturally any U-boat which sunk another ship within sight of the *Potomac* was going to be sunk by the American Navy, Doenitz had no doubts about that. The *Amis* were paranoiac about the safety of the President.

But the loss of one U-boat would be of little consequence if Churchill were sent to the bottom of the ocean and the alliance between Britain and America severed before the British could drag the *Amis* into the war.

Finally Hitler gasped for breath and stopped speaking. Von Arco didn't hesitate. 'So, *mein Führer,* we intend to concentrate every wolf pack in the whole of the Atlantic Ocean off the New England, Canadian and Newfoundland seaboard. Once the *Potomac* is located, they will devote themselves to trailing her. If one pack is located by the US Navy, then another pack will take over, but always there will be one group of U-boats following the President's ship, leading us straight to the *Prince of Wales.*' He stopped and smiled at the Führer.

'*This is absolute madness!*' Jodl snapped, clever pale face flushed with barely suppressed anger. 'We run the danger of gravely antagonising the United States – and more importantly, we are taking our U-boats out of operation just when they are most desperately needed to stop US supplies reaching England and from thence the Russians.'

But no one was listening to Colonel-General Jodl this day. All attention was concentrated on the two officers of the Submarine Service, as Hitler rapped out a series of questions, the words tumbling from his mouth excitedly, little white flecks of foam at both sides. *'When do you think Churchill will sail...? What do we know of Roosevelt's plans...? What agents have we located on America's eastern seaboard to report of sailings...? What is our present strength in the Atlantic?'* And finally that one overwhelming question which had been plaguing Doenitz ever since von Arco had brought him the intercept and made that bold suggestion: *'Will our ships reach the rendezvous in time and in full strength?'*

But the Admiral put a bold face on it. *'Mein Führer,'* he snapped, while Jodl continued to throw him vitriolic looks and Keitel, stiff and stupid, still tried to puzzle out exactly what was going on, 'if you will allow me to use your personal scrambler, I will give my staff back at Murwik the code-word which will alert every U-boat in the Atlantic Ocean and set them sailing at full speed for the other side.'

Hitler could not suppress his surprise and admiration. 'You mean you have everything worked out already, Doenitz?'

'Jawohl mein Führer!' Doenitz barked proudly. 'My staff has worked everything out to the last detail. All I was waiting for was the go-ahead from you, sir. At this very moment my people are waiting at the other end in Murwik for my signal – the code-word.'

Hitler beamed at him encouragingly. 'And

what is that particular code-word, if I may ask?'

Doenitz hesitated only an instant before he barked: 'The code-word, *mein Führer*, is Death Watch.'

'*Death Watch!*' Hitler exclaimed and clapped his hands together with delight as a small child might do. 'How apt! Watch and death – *to the Prince of Wales and Mister Winston Churchill....!*'

CHAPTER 6

'*There are no roses on a sailor's grave,*' Frenssen bellowed, face turned a brick-red by the sea-wind, '*no lilies on an ocean wave... The only tribute is the seagull's sweep ... and the teardrops that a sweetheart weeps...*' Frenssen gave a dramatic sob, the drops of seaspray trickling down his face like tears.

Christian shook his head in mock wonder and said, not taking his eyes off the horizon for a moment, 'You're in a particularly happy mood this day, *Obermaat*. Do you think you're going to snuff it soon?'

Frenssen whipped a large opaque dewdrop off the end of his big red nose and tossed it expertly over the side into the heaving waves. 'What frigging difference would it make, sir? No suds, no gash, not even a frigging kill in three weeks. Might as well be looking at the tatties from below, don't yer think?'

Jungblut's handsome young face creased into a smile. 'Suppose you're right, *Obermaat,* but where we're supposed to find suds and gash in the middle of the Atlantic Ocean, I simply wouldn't know.' Routinely he swung up his binoculars and swept the horizon. Again nothing, as usual.

Wolf Pack Thorn, commanded by Captain Thorn of U-69, had been hunting for nearly three weeks off the American Eastern Seaboard and had not had a single success in spite of the fact that there were convoys currently leaving Boston and St John's virtually every week. Every time the wolf pack had managed to get within killing range, enemy planes or destroyers had appeared and had forced the wolf pack to submerge. It was all very frustrating; and now it was nearly six days since they had last sighted an enemy ship.

'Did I ever tell you about the time I met the whore with two sets of tits on the *Reeperbahn*, Lieutenant?' Frenssen asked, abandoning his mournful sailor's song.

'Yes, *Obermaat*, but undoubtedly you're going to tell me it once again.'

The burly Hamburger did not seem to hear. Instead he launched into his story with 'Well, Lieutenant, it was like this. I was strolling down the *Reeperbahn* last year when we were having that refit ready to fall in love with any piece of gash that came my way, when I spotted this wench wilth all this wood in front of her door. I'd never seen anything like it. She had lungs on her like a ten dollar nag! Of course, I fell in love with her straight off; well, at the sight of all that meat – and no potatoes – who wouldn't? I started walking with a limp and right off–'

'*Schauze!*' Jungblut cut in harshly and flung up his glasses. The big petty officer stopped immediately and raised his own binoculars. A dark shape trailing a smudge of brown smoke behind it slid silently into the bright circle of calibrated glass. 'What do you make of it, *Obermaat?*' Jungblut rasped, his young face set and hard as he felt the old thrill of the chase beginning to surge through his body.

Frenssen, the veteran who had even fought in the Spanish Civil War and who had now survived three long years of submarine warfare, hesitated only a second before barking, 'Tommy, sir ... Tommy merchantman! Far as I can make out from her colours and rig, she's a ten thousand tonner of the Ellerman Wilson Line.'

Christian sprang into action. He hit the alert button, crying at the same time through the mike attached to his chest, 'Skipper, emergency dive! Tommy merchantman ... bearing zero forty degrees!' Then he and the rest of the watch was scurrying down the ladder of the conning tower, while the alarm bells started to jingle in ear-splitting fury.

He landed on all fours at the bottom of the tower and leapt out of the way. The conning tower had to be cleared within five seconds and the next man would be following him in exactly one and one fifth seconds; he didn't fancy having a pair of nailed seaboots stomping him.

Now all was feverish activity inside the U-69, as the ship switched from diesels to electric motors. Abruptly red lights were glowing everywhere; men, suddenly sweating with excitement, poised over their instruments.

CRASH! The hatch slammed closed with a metallic boom. *'FLOOD!'* Christian yelled, throwing his whole weight against the wheel which sealed the hatch.

'FLOOD!' the Chief Engineer, Frahm, echoed. He stood in front of the flooding table, counting off the diving tanks as they filled with seawater. 'Five ... four ... three ... two ... *both!'*

Now, as the sweating bearded ratings opened the valve levers with eager nervous hands, eyes wild with tension, the bow of the U-69 started to tilt. She began to dive. Now the whole submarine trembled and shivered like a live thing, as the electric motors raced all-out.

'Thirty-five degree load!' Frahm cried.

'Down to fifty fathoms,' Baer called a moment later, the strain all too obvious on his tough weather-beaten face, a vein ticking nervously at the side of his head as he pushed his cap from back to front ready to use the periscope.

Now the U-69 levelled out as she approached the still unsuspecting merchantman at a steady sixteen knots, the hydrophone operators already adjusting their dials, waiting to pick up their first contact with the enemy.

'Silent running,' the Skipper ordered.

Now all unnecessary talk ceased. The Skipper did not want the enemy to pick up any noise from below, and be alerted. The minutes passed in electric expectancy, the men's faces hollowed out to eerie, sick skulls in the unreal green glow. Christian, standing next to the Skipper in the control area, found himself swallowing repeatedly, as if his lungs simply could not obtain enough oxygen. It was the old tense nervousness of the pre-attack.

The first hydrophone sang out his reading and Captain Baer snapped into action. 'Take up to periscope depth,' he growled and bent expectantly, big hairy paws already on the handles of the periscope.

'Periscope depth!' the chief engineer called.

'Up periscope!' Baer commanded. Pushing his battered white cap to the back of his curly head, he peered through the tube. The crew waited tensely. Jungblut could feel a cold trickle of sweat down the small of his back. It wouldn't be long now. Baer made his decision. 'Take her up,' he ordered. 'Tubes one to four ready for surface fire!'

Now all was controlled electric activity as

the torpedo-mates prepared their deadly tin fish, two tons of high explosive, and the U-boat headed for the surface once again. Christian Jungblut bit his bottom lip with worry. He understood Baer's reasoning. He stood a better chance of hitting the enemy ship when on the surface, though at the same time, Christian knew, he was running the risk of air attack if the merchantman *did* belong to a convoy and there were escort vessels around.

Baer seemed to sense Christian's unease, for he gave that great booming laugh of his and called over his shoulder without taking his gaze off the periscope. 'Don't wet yer knickers, Number One. There hasn't been a Tommy born that could tame old Grizzly Bear!' He chuckled hugely as he used the nickname the crew gave him – behind his back. 'All right, off we go.'

Hastily Christian and the rest of the deck crew sprang into the conning tower as the U-69 broke the surface of the Atlantic. Christian opened the hatch and ducked as a shower of seawater came tumbling down. Then he and the others, followed by the somewhat more ponderous Skipper, clattered up the dripping rungs. The merchant-man was now about a kilometre away, moving on a course parallel with the U-69 and obviously still unaware that she was being shadowed by such a deadly enemy.

Captain Baer took over, after a swift glance at their victim through his binoculars. 'Ready down below,' he growled. 'Target Red 90, speed fifteen knots, range twelve hundred metres.'

He waited. Not for long. From below, the ensign in charge of the attack-table yelled upwards, 'Lined up!'

Christian flung up his binoculars. It wouldn't be long now. For a long moment he let the unsuspecting ship drift silently across the glass and, as always at this moment, he wondered about her crew, those unsuspecting fellow human beings who they would kill so startlingly in a few minutes. He shook his head hard and drove the thought away. It did not do to think too much about such things. In this year of 1941, in the Atlantic, it was kill or be killed. Here the only law was that of the jungle.

Baer felt the rising tension too. His tough, bearded face was glazed with sweat and the knuckles of his hands clutching the side of the conning tower were white, as if he were holding on for dear life. But when he spoke, his growl revealed nothing. The years of hard training and iron discipline had paid off. In the Submarine Service where men lived off their nerves for weeks on end when they were on patrol, nervous tension was something that had to be fought and suppressed. 'Commander to torpedo-officer,' he commanded. 'Stand by to fire.'

'Tubes one, three and four ready, sir!' the ensign called back.

'Commander to torpedo-officer. Fire when ready.'

'Ready!' Even though the young ensign, whose first mission this was, fought to control himself, the excitement in his voice was only too apparent.

From further down the boat, Frenssen bellowed, *'On … on … on…,'* indicating that the torpedoes' settings were correct.

The ensign waited no longer. *'FIRE!'* he shricked, voice breaking with the heady excitement of it all.

A hiss of escaping compressed air. A wild flurry of bubbles raced for the surface. A lurch as the three deadly fish left the U-boat at one-second intervals. And then the torpedoes were streaking for the merchant-man, racing for the kill. Jungblut and the Skipper adjusted their binoculars frantically while the crew below fell absolutely silent, all motionless while they waited, save the radioman who fiddled with his dials, urgently trying to pick up any signal the enemy ship might make the moment it was hit.

'One … two … three…' Captain Baer counted off the seconds. Suddenly, startlingly, there was a tremendous bang. Christian reeled back. It was as if his face had

been slapped by a soft, wet giant palm. Instinctively he opened his mouth to prevent his eardrums from being burst.

Next to him, Captain Baer yelled uproariously as the pall of smoke shot to the sky. *'Hit aft!'* he cried in triumph. 'It looks as if the stern is buckled.'

He was right; two of their torpedoes had struck home. Now the merchantman was circling lazily, purposelessly while bright cherry-red flecks of flame had started to appear in the mass of billowing, thick black smoke.

'Looks as if she's without power – and the steering mech has been hit, sir,' Christian said, watching the tiny black figures running back and forth along the stricken ship. Up front, a crew of gunners were attempting to get the vessel's single gun into action. But they hadn't a chance.

Behind Christian, *Obermaat* Frenssen, roaring 'Fie, fei, foo, fum, I smell the blood of an Englishman,' swung the conning tower's heavy machine-gun as if it were a child's toy and, without appearing to aim, whipped off a long burst.

The white and green tracer raced across the intervening sea in swift, highly-lethal morse. The gunners flung up their arms dramatically as they were hit and dropped to the deck, writhing and twitching violently, galvanised into crazy action in the last moments before death overcame them.

'Full ahead!' Baer yelled into the tube.

Below, the diesels throbbed into powerful life and the submarine surged forward for the final kill, while Frenssen tensed over the machine-gun, humming his bloody-thirsty little jingle.

The merchantman grew closer and closer. Christian could see quite clearly the panic-stricken efforts of the crew to lower a lifeboat on the port side, as they fought the jumbled, shattered rigging to free it. Again he was overcome with that old familiar emotion at the daemonic madness of destruction in the Atlantic. Even if those men fighting for their lives did manage to free the lifeboat, the crew of the U-69 would be unable to help them. U-boats were not built to accommodate those who survived. If an enemy ship didn't come across them, they would perish in the vastness of that cruel, cruel Atlantic.

'Stop both!' the Captain's voice broke into his reverie. The U-boat came slowly to a halt. Hastily Baer gave his final order. 'Range three hundred metres – *FEUER!*'

A tremendous roar. A metallic creak and the audible rending of steel plates being torn apart. The stern of the dying merchantmen reared up out of the water like a live thing, a wild horse being put to the saddle for the very first time. Steam hissed out of ruptured boilers. Great obscene bubbles of compressed air broke on the surface in a sudden flurry of wild white water.

Baer and the rest yelled in triumph. From below came the cheers of the crew as they heard the news.

Now the ship was sinking fast, poised for her last plunge. The sea air was full of the stench of escaping diesel and the fearful crics of the trapped seamen packed high on the towering stern, waving and shouting and praying for help. But this day, the God of War wasn't listening to any pleas for help. Slowly but surely, the merchantman began to disappear beneath the boiling waves, taking her crew with her. Suddenly the look of triumph vanished from Captain Baer's broad, tough face. Slowly and solemnly he raised his paw to his battered white cap in salute. 'Poor shits,' he murmured.

Behind him Frenssen nodded his head in agreement. 'We're all poor shits,' he whispered, as if talking to himself. Frenssen was right, Christian told himself: all of them who fought in the cruel Battle of the Atlantic, victor and vanquished, all of them were doomed in the end.

CHAPTER 7

The ship lay there upside down, as big as the whole world, silent now save for the occasional bubble of trapped air exploding on the surface. Gently, almost hesitantly the U-69 nosed its way through the debris: bottles, cans, a bosun's chair – *and the dead!* Charred and shrunken to the size of hideous pygmies, their skeletal fingers sticking upwards like withered twigs; a cook, perhaps, boiled alive so that his body was one massive pink blister; two lascars, with not a mark on them, but dead all the same, their lungs burst by the explosion, clasping in each other's arms like lovers in a passionate embrace; a solitary brawny arm tossing back and forth on the waves, tattooed pathetically in blue and red with the legend 'Mother'.

Frenssen shook his big head. 'No more suds and gash for him, or any of them, *Herr Leutnant.* Goes to sea all yer life, seeing yer mates die one by one, and then you end up like that.' He shook his head again. 'What a frigging life it is for yer ordinary common sailorman!' He spat morosely over the side as the arm disappeared.

Five minutes later just when Captain Baer

had decided that there was nothing of military importance to be found among the wreckage – before he had died, the unknown skipper had tossed the ship's weighed codebooks over the side obviously – there came that familiar, yet frightening call from the starboard lookout: 'Aircraft – to starboard – coming in *FAST!*'

'Damned shit!' Baer cried in anger. 'The Tommy must have warned them after all...' He reached for the klaxon and sounded that shrill warning, striking fear and terror into even the most experienced and hardened U-boat man: *'DIVE... DIVE...!'* he yelled fervently as the deck crew doubled for the conning tower and the five dark dots on the horizon raced forward, growing alarmingly larger by the instant.

The torpedo from port caught the U-boat completely by surprise. Sneaking in from out of the sun, the other enemy plane had taken them totally unawares. There was a tremendous thump. A violent tremor flashed through the submarine. It lurched crazily, its superstructure seeming to touch the waves as the stern crumpled and on all sides the screams, the shrieks for help, the sharp cries of pain rose in a terrible crescendo.

Christian found himself flung against the side of the conning tower. He howled with pain as something in his left arm snapped. In front of him in a kind of distorted, blurred vision of horror he saw the Skipper fling his big hairy paws to his stomach, from which his guts had begun to slip out, a steaming terrifying snake of pulsating slimy grey. Next to him the face of one of the watchkeepers was streaming down to his chest like dreadful red molten wax, taking the features with it.

For one moment he blacked out and went down on his knees like a boxer trying to fight off a count of ten. He shook his head, hard. It hurt. But everything came back into focus. The dying Skipper, the dive bomber soaring high into the blue sky, the squadron of ponderous four-engined seaplanes winging ever closer. He knew he must take over, force himself to act. Time was running out for the U-69 *rapidly!*

He staggered to his feet, trying to blot out the screams and moans of the wounded. 'Quick, Frenssen, get the Skipper down below... At the double, man!'

'At the double, sir!' Hastily Frenssen wiped the blood from his nose and chin and then lifting the dying Captain, as if he were a baby, he staggered down below.

Wildly Christian flung a glance down the length of the U-69. A dead sailor lay crumpled near the bow gun, but otherwise the hull looked all right. But the stern was in a terrible mess, the plates cracked and buckled, with smoke escaping from the diesels through the gaps. Dare he attempt to dive with the ship in such a state? Wouldn't he be taking her right down to the bottom of the Atlantic Ocean?

Now the flying boats were almost upon them. In a matter of minutes they'd be smothering the area in depth-charges. There was no other way. He had to chance it. As the last of the deck crew hit the bottom of the conning tower and the thunder of the planes rose to an ear-splitting pitch, he flung himself down the ladder, riding it with both feet, crying wildly as he did so, *'Dive ... dive ... dive!'*

Madly he spun the hatch closed in the same instant that the engineer officer started to take her down and the first depth-charges began hitting the sea where they had just been. The ordeal had commenced.

Yet another salvo of depth-charges hit the surface above them. Four short, ferocious explosions shattered the water all around them. The boat shuddered violently. With a sudden sinking lurch the U-69 fell sixty degrees. Water spurted everywhere through the shattered plates. The steel shrieked wildly under the almost unbearable pressure. Valves blew. Deck plates sprang upwards. The lights went out.

For one awful moment Christian almost lost his nerve there in the stinking darkness, with the wounded crying out in alarm and the dying Captain moaning: 'Old Grizzly Bear won't let you down, lads... Never worry, Old Grizzly Bear...'

The lights flicked on again and the hydroplane operators, their singlets black with sweat, their faces greased as if with Vaseline, whirled their wheels furiously to restore the battered U-boat's trim.

They had been under attack for nearly thirty minutes, which had to be beyond the flying time of the average flying boat; but a harassed, worried Christian, staring now at the shambles of the U-69, reasoned that the first flight had dropped a smoke marker and the attack had been taken up by another group of the damned enemy planes.

Christian crooked a finger at Ensign Hinrichs, his face pale and worried. They were rigged for silent running and Christian wanted as little noise as possible in case enemy surface vessels were already on the scene. 'Take over, Hinrichs,' he whispered. 'I'm going to have a look at Grizzly Bear and check out the boat... And don't look so worried,' he added with more conviction than he felt, 'we'll get through and you're doing fine.'

Hinrichs swallowed hard, eyes wide and wild with fear. 'Thank you, sir!' he croaked.

Hastily Christian patted him on the arm and staggered through the debris and foul, oil-scummed water washing over the deck to where the Skipper lay, cradled in a sodden mess of blankets and life-jackets. Now his breathing was hectic and very shallow and there was an odd pinched, white look about the tip of his nose, which Christian knew always indicated the approach of death. Someone had slapped a large shell dressing on across his shattered intestines, but it was already crimson with new blood. Reluctantly but knowing he must do so, Christian turned the dying man round as gently as he could, while Frenssen watched from above. Carefully he lowered the Skipper's trousers. The seat was thick with jellied blood and as he lifted up the Skipper's shirt, he could see that his hairy buttocks were matted with more of the same. Captain Baer was bleeding internally.

Solemnly Frenssen shook his head, as Christian pulled the trousers back up again.

Sadly Christian nodded his agreement, then he dismissed the dying Skipper. Now his first responsibility was to the living. 'What's she look like, *Obermaat?*' he asked softly, then grabbed suddenly for a stanchion as the boat rocked violently once more and was sent plunging deeper, causing rudder and hydroplanes to block in the extreme position. For one awesome, breathtaking moment it seemed that nothing would stop the U-69 plunging right to the bottom of the Atlantic. Confusion and panic reigned, but suddenly Ensign Hinrichs was bellowing orders above the racket and the ratings were scuttling through the chaos to restore the trim. Slowly but surely the U-69 levelled out once more.

Christian breathed a heart-felt sigh of relief. 'Another one of those and I swear I'll fill my pants.'

Frenssen laughed cynically. 'To put it politely, sir, the ordure has been trickling down my right flipper for some considerable time now!'

'Report!' Christian snapped, businesslike once again.

'All the batteries for the electric motors are leaking, sir. Doubt if we've got more than two hours submerged sailing left.'

'Oxygen?'

'About the same, sir.'

Christian considered for a moment, the only sound the steady *drip-drip* of the leaking plates and the moans of the wounded, staring at the yellow, glazed, tense faces of the men whose lives now rested in his hands.

Frenssen watched him. At twenty-three *Leutnant zur See* Christian Jungblut was a veteran. His handsome face under the cropped blond hair was tough and determined, the blue eyes firm and purposeful. He radiated assurance and determination.

He had the look of a fighter in his prime about him. Yet all the same, the decisions he had to make were almost unbearable for a man of his age. 'Frau Frenssen's handsome son certainly wouldn't like to have to make them, no sir!' he thought to himself.

'So we can stay submerged for two hours, perhaps three if we use the masks and don't run the electric motors. Then we have to surface. And if they are still waiting for us up there?'

Frenssen shrugged his brutally muscled shoulders. 'The Tommies, or whoever the apeturds up there are, will make mincemeat of us, sir.'

Christian nodded his agreement. 'That's about it, isn't it? If we stay down we croak from lack of oxygen – and if we go up, they'll drop a very nasty square egg on our turnips.' He extended his hands a little helplessly. *'So oder so – kaput!'*

Again the silent boat lurched under shattering blows that sounded like a gigantic steel club thrashing a sheet of iron. Next to Christian, squatting on the littered deck, Ensign Hinrichs gasped and croaked, for now their oxygen was very low, 'God in Heaven, will they never give up, sir?'

Christian shook his head slowly, knowing that any swift movement just ate up the precious oxygen more quickly. 'No, they know we're down here all right. They're not going to let up until they've sunk us.'

'What about darkness, sir? Couldn't we escape under the cover of darkness, sir?'

'No. There are still two hours till nightfall and our oxygen will have failed long–'

'*Herr Leutnant!*' It was Frenssen, his voice urgent and demanding.

Christian swung round. The Skipper still lay in a pool of bright-red blood and sea-water, but he was conscious again, weakly beckoning to his young Number One. There was something about his expression, a mixture of pathos, urgency and cunning, that made Christian forget his despair and lethargy. He was across like a shot. 'What is it, sir?' he demanded, while Frenssen supported the Skipper's head tenderly.

Grizzly Bear tried to smile but failed miserably. 'Christian, you've got to take her up ... there's so little time left.' Christian opened his mouth to say something, but the dying officer shook his head weakly for him to remain silent. 'Listen, it's an old trick, but it ... might work... Waste oil, all the spare clothes the crew can find ... and ... a body...'

'*A body?*' Christian echoed.

'Yes ... that should prove it to them, Christian... If there was ... a body.' The dying Skipper coughed thickly. What came up was tinged a bright pink.

94

'But sir,' he protested incredulously, wondering if the Skipper was already fantasizing. 'We haven't got ... a body!'

It seemed to take the Skipper a long time to answer. His lips trembled and the mouth moved, but no words came out. All around in the green-glowing fetid hell of the trapped submarine, the exhausted, sweat-lathered crew craned their necks to hear what the dying captain had to say.

Suddenly Baer's face creased into a weary smile. 'Christian,' he said so weakly that the latter had to lean forward almost to his head to hear what he was saying. Now a thin trickle of dark red blood was beginning to dribble from the corner of his mouth, staining his beard. 'Body ... now you have ... your ... body.' He choked. Abruptly, startlingly, his head fell to one side, the light gone from his eyes. Captain Baer, known as Grizzly Bear, was dead!

For a long, long time no one moved inside the trapped submarine. Like actors frozen there in their melodramatic positions, waiting for the curtain to go down before they could move once more, they waited.

Outside the depth-charges exploded once more, the blast rapping the hull like the tapping of some gigantic beak. Here and there new leaks sprang up. Still no one made a move.

It was when Frenssen finally slipped his thumbs across the dead Skipper's face and closed his eyes that the spell was at last broken.

Suddenly Christian Jungblut was aware that they were all staring at him expectantly. He knew why: Baer was dead; now he was the Skipper. It was up to him to rescue the U-69 and all those who sailed in her, if he could. His eyes sparkling with tears, Christian took one last look at Grizzly Bear's still, suddenly wan and sunken face and began to issue his orders...

BOOK TWO

The Race for the Shore

'Mr Winston S. Churchill must not die on the soil or in the waters of the North American continent.'

Chief-Inspector MacKenzie of the Royal Canadian Mounted Police to President Roosevelt, August 1941

CHAPTER 1

Von Arco clattered up the stairs of the big apartment house, not giving a damn whether Frau Doktor Dietz on the second floor heard him or not. What did he care about the precious reputations of these war widows? The whole lot of them were nothing better than whores.

He pressed the button marked: *Frau Kapitänleutnant Ilse Hirsch (widowed)*. Suddenly his heart was beating excitedly and he knew it was not because of the rush from HQ and then the stairs.

Ilse, plump, pale and very blonde, opened it immediately, as if she had been waiting behind the big white door all the time. She looked decidedly fetching, he told himself, in her simple black frock. She was still in mourning, even though at least half a dozen other officers had been up her skirts since it had been officially declared that her husband Klaus had died 'heroically for Folk, Fatherland and Führer' somewhere in the North Atlantic. 'It's you!' she gasped somewhat stupidly, 'I thought you—'

He didn't give her time to finish. Eyes gleaming with excitement, he thrust her inside and slammed the door closed behind him with the heel of his foot. Almost immediately he grasped her plump breasts and squeezed them, commanding hoarsely, 'Get your clothes off ... I've only got an hour!' He started pulling off his elegant tunic. 'Let's get in the sack... Quick!'

'But Kuno,' she protested, 'it's only one o'clock in the afternoon! Perhaps that old bitch Dietz will hear the bedsprings going and–'

He thrust his hand up her short skirt: up beyond the top of the black stockings into the soft, secret flesh beyond. She sighed and her eyes half closed, mouth open and gasping, almost as if she were in pain. 'Oh, Kuno,' she sighed. *'Kuno....!'*

He released her and began taking the rest of his clothes off while she did the same, her face a mixture of hesitancy and anticipation. He watched, noting how her breasts were delightfully full, the nipples already big with excitement as she released them from her black brassiere. Then he looked in triumph at the photograph of her late husband taken on the bridge of his U-boat before he had sailed away for good. 'I'll give her an extra thrust for you, dear Klaus,' he said mockingly to himself. He had always hated Klaus Hirsch for all those 'kills' of his and the fact that he had been received by the Führer three times. Then he could wait no longer.

He reached out, ripped her black panties from her, lifted her in his arms the very next moment and tumbled her, a mass of flailing arms, legs, breasts, onto the big double bed. She yelped with pleasure.

'You've got twenty minutes left, darling,' Ilse whispered lovingly, looking down at his handsome face now glazed with sweat, as if someone had covered it with Vaseline. Kuno looked absurdly young and vulnerable. Her husband had always looked very fierce and frightening afterwards, as he might do just before he was to inspect his crew. She stroked his face tenderly.

Von Arco awoke immediately. 'What did you say?' he said thickly.

'Twenty minutes left, lover,' she said softly and stroked him again, nuzzling her right breast against the side of his face.

He brushed her away and said: 'You were really very good this time, Ilse. Very exciting, very pleasing. Pass over a lung torpedo, will you please?'

She smiled sweetly and passed him the cigarette he wanted from the bedside, but inside her heart sank. He talked of the act of love as if it were a commodity: one of those hearty sailors' meals of red cabbage and smoked pork that her husband had always demanded when he returned from a patrol. Suddenly Ilse Hirsch felt unhappy.

Hastily von Arco took a few puffs of his cigarette and then stabbed it out almost angrily. 'All right, Ilse, don't waste time. My orderly will be here in twenty minutes with the car. Come on, play with it...'

Ten minutes later he was clattering down the stairs, not giving a damn if that cow Dietz saw him or not, and out in the street, where the orderly stood rigidly to attention holding the door of the big staff car. Ilse sighed and let the lace curtain slip back. Abruptly she saw the rest of her life before her. Von Arco would go, but there would be others. Solemn or drunken, calm or desperate, fanatical or cynical, a whole line of them bolting through her bedroom before they disappeared for good and each with the haunted look of men facing sudden death. Ilse sat down on the rumpled bed suddenly, the tears coursing down her plump, pretty, silly face unheeded...

Doenitz wasted no time as he paced up and down in the big echoing operations room like a caged animal, impatient to be set free. 'Von Arco,' he barked as soon as the former had reported in, 'things are starting to move. We have received reports from agents that the American Harry Hopkins, Roosevelt's personal envoy, has flown to Scapa Flow from Moscow. It is obvious why.'

It was not a question. It was a statement

and von Arco snapped briskly. 'Yessir. It's from Scapa Flow that they – Churchill and Hopkins – will sail for America on board the *Prince of Wales.*'

'Exactly. Our agents in the United States also report that the press are floating rumours over there that – I quote – "a high British personage" is expected there soon by air. Swiss radio has also reported from Berne that it is rumoured the drunken sot Churchill is meeting the Jew Roosevelt soon. In short, *the meeting is on!*'

Von Arco beamed at his chief. 'Excellent news, sir. Operation Death Watch can move into stage red.'

'I have already given the order this very morning for it to do so,' Doenitz snapped, but he did not return the other's smile. His hatchet face remained hard and inflexible. 'But there are problems with our wolf packs.'

'Problems, sir?' Von Arco's smile vanished.

'Yes. As you know, Thorn lost the U-23 at the start of the operation. Now we have not heard from the U-69 since the day before yesterday. Wolf Pack Hartmann is also experiencing difficulties. Yesterday we were only receiving weak signals from them. This morning we have received nothing. Only Wolf Pack Heinz seems still to have its full complement of craft and is reporting in regularly. In other words, von Arco,' Doenitz, his rat-trap of a mouth working as if on steel springs, 'our forces which will carry out this bold plan appear to be highly disorganized. And I shall tell you why. Communications are stretched to almost breaking point! Nearly five thousand kilometres separate them from HQ. It is not surprising that we find it so difficult to co-ordinate operations.' He paused and let his words sink in, staring at the big battle-map of the Atlantic, festooned with taut coloured ribbons and a rash of blue and red china pencil marks.

Von Arco stared with him, his ego suddenly deflated. Was the grand scheme which would make him an admiral going to fall through after all? Was all the scheming and planning going to be for nothing? What a piggery it was! Those 'heroes of the Atlantic', as the popular press called the U-boat captains, were a hopeless lot. They deserved to go down with their damned subs!

'All this morning,' Doenitz resumed, speaking more slowly than usual, as if he were thinking out his new plan as he spoke, 'I have been giving this problem of co-ordinating Operation Death Watch a great deal of thought. I have come to the conclusion, as this is an operation of an absolutely different kind to any the Submarine Service has yet carried out in this war, that it must be co-ordinated and directed by an experienced staff officer from the other side' – he hesitated only momentarily – *'of the Atlantic!'*

Von Arco stared at the Admiral in wild-eyed disbelief. 'From the other side of the Atlantic, sir?' he echoed, completely dumbfounded by this new development. 'But how, sir...? *Where?*'

Surprisingly for such a supreme realist, Admiral Doenitz played coy. Instead of answering von Arco's question directly, he said: 'You know the problem that we have had ever since the start of this war in predicting the weather over Britain and the Atlantic, don't you, von Arco?'

Von Arco nodded warily. He did. Each bombing raid, every naval action, commando raid, parachute drop, depended upon reliable information about the weather and the weather in Western Europe could only be forecast if the military meteorologists had prior information of what was happening everywhere in the Arctic Circle to the west. As a result, secret teams of German naval specialists and scientists had been landed by U-boat all over the area, from Franz Josef Land, which belonged to the Russians, to East Greenland, which came under Danish control. Here over the last three years a strange, lonely war had been fought between the Germans and, at varying times, patrols from the Russian, Norwegian, Danish, Canadian and British Armies. It was a cat-and-mouse campaign with small groups of highly skilled and very tough men hunting

GERMAN BAY SUMMER 1941

GERMANY

NORWAY

Arctic Circle

BRITISH ISLES

ICELAND

GREENLAND

Atlantic Ocean

GERMAN BAY

NEWFOUNDLAND

Placentia Bay

CANADA

each other over thousands of square kilometres of snow and ice, with the Western Allies trying to root out each new secret radio station as soon as they had located it.

As soon as one station was discovered and closed by the Allies, another was set up by men prepared to spend months, perhaps even years, cut off from the Fatherland, living under the hardest conditions imaginable in that savage northern wilderness.

Doenitz allowed the bewildered staff officer time to think the matter over and presumably wonder what the weather station problem had to do with Operation Death Watch before saying: 'Much valuable time and many good men have been lost in weather station operations. Last spring, however, Berlin discovered that it had the answer to the problem right under its very nose. A purpose-built weather station in an area of northern Canada where the enemy would never suspect in a million years that our people were located. Have you ever heard of German Bay, von Arco?'

'No, sir.'

'Very few people have – fortunately.' He chuckled suddenly but there was no warmth in his laugh. 'German Bay, yes, *nomen est omen*. You see German Bay has been inhabited by German stock for nearly two hundred years now, a little island of German language and culture and, above all,' he raised his finger warningly, 'German spirit and loyalty for two centuries. A perfect place for us to hide a weather station, what?'

Von Arco looked impressed; he *was* impressed. 'Why, sir, it's perfect!'

'It is *absolutely* perfect! Come over here. Let me show you the place on the map.'

Together they crossed to the huge wall-map of the Atlantic. Taking a pointer, Doenitz traced a route from the exit to the Baltic, by the Faroes, on to Iceland, sweeping south to Newfoundland.

Von Arco watched mesmerized, asking himself what the Big Lion was up to. What new secret was he going to reveal and what had it to do with him?

The pointer continued across the Atlantic from Iceland, sweeping by St John's in Newfoundland and finally coming to rest in a massive bay. 'Placentia Bay,' he announced, and gave von Arco the benefit of his cold smile. He moved his pointer across the waterway slightly, to the western shore on the Canadian side of the bay. 'With here – German Bay.'

Doenitz allowed von Arco time to stare intently at the map and note that the area was very thinly settled and that, indeed, the village of German Bay was very isolated, before he started to explain: 'After the American revolution against the English in the 18th century, von Arco, many of the new

Squids in: R

...dd dog biscuits
...opping list.

📧 **vitalityhealth.co.uk/echodot** ☎ **0808 274 3040**

Vitality
HEALTH INSURANCE

Americans voted with their feet. Those who could not swear allegiance to the Stars and Stripes – they called them the Empire Loyalists – moved north to form new communities in Canada, which had remained loyal to England. Now among those Empire Loyalists, there were a small group of German mercenaries from the King's German Legion which had fought on the side of the English against the colonialists. In return for their services they had been promised a pension by King George III and land in America on which to settle. After the English had lost the war against the Americans that was, of course, out of the question. They were hated bitterly by the Americans. The Empire Loyalists didn't like them very much either. They regarded the Germans as foreigners and cruel hired mercenaries.

'So they set themselves up in that isolated area, away from the rest of the emigrants, making a poor living from fishing and what they could scratch from the land, which was – and still is – poor. A peasant and farming community, in other words, von Arco, which kept very close to itself, sticking to its own ways and customs and maintaining our noble language.' He paused momentarily. 'And positioned right on the edge of a splendid deep fiord ideally suited to our purposes,' he added with a significant nod of his head.

'Our purposes, sir?' von Arco echoed more

puzzled than ever. 'How do you mean, sir?'

But von Arco was not destined to have that particular question answered just then, for in that very moment there came a sudden urgent knocking on the big door of the Map Room.

'*Herein!*' Doenitz barked and spun round, for he knew it must be something important for anyone to disturb *him* in conference.

It was the signals officer who had translated for von Arco in the cipher room. He was flushed and not a little excited as he clicked to attention, radio message held in a hand that trembled slightly.

'Well?' Doenitz snapped.

'It's the U-69, sir. We've just made contact with her, sir.' He beamed at his two superiors as if it gave him personal pleasure to know the submarine had not been sent to the bottom of the Atlantic – this time. 'She has not been sunk after all. She is badly damaged and her captain has been killed. She is now commanded by a' – he flung a quick glance at the radio message – '*Leutnant zur See* Jungblut, who now asks for permission to return home.'

Doenitz's face flushed an angry red. 'By God, *no!*' he cried and slammed his clenched fist down hard on the table. 'Now you see why, von Arco, I need a co-ordinating officer on the other side of the Atlantic!'

Von Arco's heart sank abruptly and he felt

110

a cold finger of fear trace its way down the small of his back. He knew who was going to be that co-ordinating officer – and he was afraid.

CHAPTER 2

The sole surviving diesel began its monotonous drone once more. All around the Atlantic was calm and unruffled. Men off duty lay naked on the deck, their pallid bodies slowly beginning to turn brown in the July sun. Watching them, Christian told himself that it was good for them. Their haggard, pinched look had begun to disappear and the sun's rays certainly were the best cure for the rashes and sores that afflicted most of them after four weeks of cruising underwater.

At the bow a few of the more adventurous souls had made themselves rough wooden surf-boards and, attached by ropes held by their comrades, they were chortling and laughing as they rode with the bow wave. It was all very calm and restful after the tension and even Christian relaxed a little, wondering when permission would come through for him to bring the damaged U-69 back to port for repairs and the whole dangerous business of attempting to sail from the North Sea into the safety of the Baltic would commence once more.

Beside him Frenssen, stripped completely naked save for a pistol belt, the sign of his authority as Chief Petty Officer, routinely punched little holes in the soles of a brand-new pair of seaboots. The greenhorns stared at him, not daring to ask, but wondering all the same why the *Obermaat* was systematically ruining a pair of boots. Christian knew. All the veterans did it. Over the hours of a long and wet deck watch boots slowly filled up with water, turning the feet into blocks of ice. Soon, after a few days of water-logged boots, the feet would turn into wrinkled, swollen monstrosities, requiring medical treatment for a kind of marine trench-foot. By punching the soles full of holes, the water was allowed to run off and the feet remained relatively dry. Soon, after a few watches in one of those terrible North Atlantic rain-storms, the greenhorns would be doing it too.

Frenssen was well aware of the curious gazes of the new men and, in the way of the old hares, always ready to take a rise out of 'greenbeaks', as they were called contemptuously, he said in a casual way: 'Did I ever tell you bunch of piss-pansies about the time when I was just gonna slap my cele-brated piece of hard salami into a five-mark whore in Kiel, eh?'

The greenbeaks, innocents that they were in spite of their constant boasting about their mighty sexual prowess, shook their cropped heads in unison.

'Well, it was like this. I was just about to rip her skivvies down, open them pearly gates and treat her to the best piece o' salami that pavement pounder ever experienced in a lifetime of dancing the mattress polka, when she sez to me, "Hold hard, sailor boy. Like to try something new? I bet yer ain't ever had this before." "Like what, missus?" sez I, put off me stroke. *"Malaria perhaps?"'* He chortled hugely at what he thought was a wicked piece of humour.

The greenbeaks craned closer. 'And what did she do, *Obermaat?'* one of the innocents asked eagerly.

'I'll tell yer laddie, she whipped out her right eyeball. It was made of glass, yer see.'

The greenbeaks gasped.

'And then she said, "If yer really want something new, sailor, stick it in there!"'

'But what for, *Obermaat?'* the greenbeaks yelled in unison.

'What for, yer ask, you lot of cardboard sailors?' Frenssen shouted. 'Why – *to wink me off!'* he bellowed and broke into uproarious laughter. *'To wink me off!'*

Christian shook his head in mock wonder, as Frenssen clutched his stomach, overcome by so much laughter, the tears streaming down his red face. But Frenssen's crude sexual humour was part and parcel of the rough, brutal and sometimes short life most of the U-boat sailors led: waterfront brothels

114

from Bergen to Brest, stinking of sweat, semen and cheap scent. Whores, flaccid cylinders of flesh, for them to relieve themselves. Man after man. Cynical, bored whores staring at the dirty flyblown ceiling, smoking as the men pounded at them. Afterwards the sickbay, stinking of lysol, with the attendants squirting yellow slime up their penises. Outside and into the night, staggering from cheap bar to bar, swilling down the local rotgut, spending the accumulated pay from a long cruise, paying for rounds for the bands, lighting cigars with twenty mark notes, tipping the freaks outrageously; the man who ate razor blades, the fat woman who had a rat tattooed on her enormous buttocks as if it were entering her anus, the old man who had no penis... Until they had just enough left to pay the taxi-driver to unload them at their ship, drunk beyond reason. And for a while the dread memories were blotted out. But only for a while. Always it began again, until one day there came that last patrol, from which there was no return.

He dismissed that particular gloomy subject and concentrated on enjoying the sun as well as keeping the watch. The U-69 had suffered considerable damage during that last terrible attack in which Captain Baer had died. They had managed to recharge the batteries of the electric motors and repair them, but the damaged diesel was beyond their present capacity. They had managed to patch up the damaged hull, too, but it would not stand any real deep diving. So Christian had steered the U-69 away from the main enemy shipping lanes where they could expect attack from enemy escort vessels. Here they were relatively safe, save perhaps for some enemy reconnaissance plane flying over the endless ocean from Iceland.

Already he had a course planned out for the damaged ship which would allow it to limp along for most of the return home on the surface. Once they entered the North Sea he would submerge and hope that his electric motors would hold out until they had safely passed those highly dangerous narrows between Denmark and Norway.

Now, however, the U-69 was sailing in a kind of limbo in these remote waters, waiting for orders while they enjoyed the sun and told their old, old yarns about tremendous binges and astonishing feats of sexual prowess. For a while this was a time out of war for the crew of the battered U-69. But it would not last long…

It was twenty-four hours later, after they had first reported their position, that the radio operators down below first started to decode the radio message from Murwik. Above, in the bright sunshine, the rest had almost completed the task given to them by

Christian, namely to rig up some sort of camouflage for the U-69 so that it would appear from a distance like a harmless cargo boat. They had stretched pieces of linen and sail-cloth the length of both sides of the battered hull. Then they had rigged up a funnel by cutting up a sheet of tin and planting it on top of an open case with an oily rag in it. This was connected to a compressed air tube. Whenever another craft hove into sight the compressed air would enable them to jet a series of fiery-red sparks and a great deal of oily smoke upwards from the 'funnel'.

'As I see it, Ensign,' Christian said to Hinrichs, who had now turned a brilliant lobster-red in the sun, 'this way we can stay on the surface and save our electric batteries. They'll take us for some old tub of a cargo steamer.'

'Ay,' Frenssen said sourly, 'that is if they're a dozen kilometres away and need their glassy orbits testing.'

Christian laughed easily, well pleased with his creation. 'Don't be such a misery, Frenssen. With a bit of luck we'll be able to sail undetected right into the North Sea and won't have to waste fuel dodging any more ships. It'll be nip-and-tuck, but I think our diesel'll last till we reach the place where we'll dive.'

'Sir!' an urgent voice cut into the lazy chatter, rising above the noise made by the rating hammering more tin plate to make an aft mast of the kind carried by merchantmen.

Christian spun round. It was the leading radioman, face flushed with excitement and apprehension. 'Where's the fire, Jansen?'

'Straight from HQ, sir,' the radioman replied and thrust the message, as if it were red-hot, into Christian's hand. 'Top priority, sir. Did the decode myself.' He bit his bottom lip, as if worried, suddenly. 'Hope I didn't muck it up, sir. Sounds a bit strange to me...' He stopped abruptly and wiped the sweat from the palms of his hands on his overalls.

Christian's gaze flashed swiftly over the neatly printed message, the surprise on his handsome young face growing by the instant. 'Damn ... damn ... damn!' he cursed suddenly, and still holding the message walked to the edge of the conning tube, his features abruptly set and hard.

'What is it, sir?' Frenssen was first to react. Next to him the Ensign added, 'Bad news, sir?'

Christian swung round upon them. 'Yes, bad news indeed, Hinrichs. Our request to proceed home to repair and refit has been turned down!'

Frenssen gasped. 'But they can't do that, sir,' he exploded. 'Why, the boat is leaking at every seam and the diesels are shot–'

Christian held up his hand to stop him. 'I know all that and so does HQ. But we are to remain on station, sailing a westerly course along the sixtieth parallel.'

Both Hinrichs and Frenssen looked shocked. 'But sir,' the Ensign protested, 'a course of that kind would take us right into enemy waters!'

Christian nodded sombrely. 'There is more to come,' he said, trying to restrain his mounting anger against what seemed to him to be senseless orders, 'we are to proceed along the coast of Canada to roughly the fifty-third parallel, where,' he hesitated only a fraction of a second, 'where we will be met–'

'*Met!*' Frenssen yelled. 'Met by who? *The frigging King of Canada?*'

'Not exactly. It is a kind of guide-boat. It will guide us into Placentia Bay.'

'And what are we supposed to do there, sir?' Frenssen asked.

'There, apparently, repairs will be carried out before we receive further orders for a new op.'

'But sir,' Hinrichs protested. 'I hope I've got my North American geography right, but isn't Placentia Bay a kind of death-trap for a submarine? I mean, it is fringed by Newfoundland and Canada, with only two exits to the north and to the south, both narrow strips of water, easily controlled from St John's or the Canadian mainland. I should think it is a difficult place to get into and even more difficult to get out of once an anti-sub alert is sounded.'

'You've got your geography all correct, Hinrichs,' Christian said grimly. 'To my way of thinking, entering that place is an invitation to disaster.' He frowned at the crumpled message.

'Who signed a damnfool order like that, sir?' Frenssen broke the heavy silence on the bridge finally. 'Surely not the Big Lion?'

'No, it wasn't the Big Lion, admittedly,' Christian conceded grudgingly. 'But it has to have his approval. No, the order was signed by – can't you guess, Frenssen?'

'*Kapitänleutnant von Arco?*'

Christian nodded. 'No other.'

'That explains it, doesn't it, sir,' Frenssen said bitterly. 'While we're sweating it out in this battered old tub, he's sitting pretty back there, living like a fat cat, nice and safe five thousand kilometres away.' He spat sourly over the side. 'One law for the poor, one law for the rich, fuck it!'

But *Obermaat* Frenssen was mistaken. *Kapitänleutnant* von Arco's days of 'living like a fat cat, nice and safe five thousand kilometres away' were over for a while. Von Arco was closer, much closer, at that moment than a disgusted Frenssen could ever have imagined...

CHAPTER 3

The huge four-engined Focke Condor started to lose altitude now. As it did, the attentive steward waddled forward in his thick furs and bellowed in von Arco's ear: 'You can remove your oxygen mask now, sir. It's quite safe.'

Gratefully von Arco did so and rubbed the stubble of his beard which had been painfully irritated by having to wear the mask for nearly three hours while they flew high over Iceland, out of reach of English fighters. He sighed pleasurably.

It was thirteen hours now since they had set off from Bergen in Norway to fly on this long mysterious mission in the white-painted, long-range reconnaissance plane. Von Arco stretched his stiffened limbs and told himself that they would soon be making landfall. Though the thought of what might meet him there did not make him particularly happy. The whole damnfool scheme was highly dangerous, in his opinion, and Kuno von Arco had a very healthy respect for the safety of his own skin.

'Newfoundland, von Arco! Can you see it? Over there – that smudge on the horizon

121

below the port engine.'

It was the second pilot, a casual, smiling 25-year-old, to whom von Arco had taken an instinctive dislike. The fellow was too friendly, too casual and he was already the same rank as von Arco, although he was at least five years younger. But then the *Luftwaffe* was never very fussy who it promoted to officer rank.

'Isn't it dangerous, *Herr Hauptmann*,' he asked, a little apprehensively, 'to fly over the place?'

The young pilot shook his head happily. 'Not at all, von Arco. They've got a couple of popguns at St John's and a couple of antiquated biplanes, that's all. Easy as falling off a log.'

Von Arco relaxed a little, as the isolated peninsula loomed every larger. But he was still worried about the landing in Canada, where he would meet this mysterious Dr Ritter, who had set up the whole strange business at German Bay. 'I still can't understand how you're going to get away with it, *Herr Hauptmann,* landing a machine of this size on enemy territory without being detected,' he said, putting his fears into words.

The blond pilot smiled down at him and told himself the elegant boy in blue had really got the wind up! He was shit-scared! 'Nothing to it,' he answered airily. 'My God, von Arco, if you only knew some of the little larks we've gotten up to in these last few years, yer golden locks'd perm themselves!'

Von Arco frowned. He didn't like that kind of flippant talk one bit, but as his life depended upon these sloppy, careless excuses for officers, he held his peace.

'This one is going to be easy. You see, von Arco, back in forty, the *Amis* and the Canadians secretly built a field in the hills just north of German Bay to ferry aircraft *secretly* to the English in that little arsehole of an Island of theirs. Up there, they thought, nobody would ever be aware of what they were doing.'

Von Arco flushed. 'That damned Jew Roosevelt will do anything to help the decadent English!' he snorted angrily. 'Imagine a neutral America supplying our enemies with arms like that.'

'I always thought the Roosevelts were of Dutch extraction,' the second pilot answered easily and added for no other reason than to offend him, von Arco couldn't help thinking later. 'I once had a Jewish girl from Frankfurt. Wow, did she have hot pants! There's many a time I thought it was going to fall off.' He sighed fondly. 'Happy days! Well, now that the Americans are openly supplying the Tommies with planes etc under this Lease-Lend scheme of Roosevelt's, there's no need for them to hide the business. They fly the stuff straight to England from the United

States. So that leaves us with a perfectly decent field in the middle of nowhere, with not a living soul within fifty square kilometres. Of course,' he added with a malicious smile, 'now that there are no services there any more, control towers, flare paths etc, it can get a little hairy, if the fog comes in – which it does a lot in this particular part of the world.'

'Hairy?' von Arco asked nervously, flashing a glance out of the port-hole, as if he half-expected to see a massive peasouper out there.

'Blind flying by instruments. Low level stuff. Tree-hopping, that kind of thing. But now you must excuse me. I've got to relieve the chief pilot. At this time of day, he usually likes to start hitting the sauce, especially if we've got a hairy one in front of us.'

'You mean drinking – *now?*' von Arco exclaimed wildly. But already the second pilot was working his way up the fuselage and the Condor was beginning to lose height rapidly...

Herr Doktor Ritter is the agent's name,' Doenitz had explained afterwards, once the decision had been made. 'That is what he calls himself. I doubt if anyone knows his real name, even Father Christmas. All that *is* known about him is that he is our most trusted agent in the whole of North America.'

'I see, sir,' von Arco had said routinely, his mind still racing at the thought that he was now going to be sent on the highly dangerous mission to German Bay.

'It was a year ago while he was following up this business of the damned Americans' secret supplies to the English that he came across the isolated German community at German Bay. It struck him immediately that it would be an ideal place for a secret met station. The inhabitants responded at once. Their patriotic German feelings – and a certain amount of hard cash – helped.' Doenitz cleared his throat discreetly. 'It was when I read the first reports of our teams out there that it struck me that German Bay would make not only an ideal met station, but also, von Arco, the best base possible for Operation Death Watch. Our boats can be refuelled from there, there are deep caves which provide safe anchorage away from prying eyes and naturally it is the ideal spot for you to co-ordinate the operation, eh?'

'Yessir, an ideal spot,' von Arco agreed, forcing an enthusiastic smile, though at that moment he had never felt less like smiling. 'I will deem it an honour to conduct the attack on the Anglo-Americans from there.'

'Of course,' Doenitz had mused, stroking his square chin, 'once the operation has been *successfully* carried out, there will be no future for the German Bay base. Undoubtedly the enraged English will wipe it off the face of the earth. But that is a small price to be paid for the success of an operation of such magnitude!'

It was then that von Arco realized that the Big Lion was prepared to gamble all on the success of Death Watch. He would willingly sacrifice the lives of every inhabitant of German Bay to achieve his aim. Not only their lives, but those of the men of the wolf packs as well, if he could only sink the *Prince of Wales* with Churchill aboard. '*Jawohl*, Kuno,' a frightened little voice within him whispered chillingly, '*and your life, too...*'

Now the Condor was flying across the sound which separated Newfoundland from Canada, dragging its shadow behind it over sparkling blue water, devoid of any craft whatsoever. Beyond loomed the dark barren cliffs of the land, again empty of human habitation so that it seemed that they were entering a lost world as yet undiscovered by man.

'Arsehole of the world, what?' the young *Luftwaffe* captain broke into von Arco's reverie. 'Grizzly bears and salmon that's all – and not a single knocking shop for over a hundred square kilometres. God!' he shuddered melodramatically. 'Fancy that, von Arco, a land without gash!'

Von Arco ignored the comment. 'When do

we land, *Herr Hauptmann?*' he began, then stopped suddenly as he spotted the first wisps of grey fog beginning to curl themselves around the peaks like silent cats. 'I say, is that fog?' he demanded urgently.

The Captain nodded, the usual grin suddenly absent from his face. 'I would say that you might be right, von Arco. It *is* frigging fog! Oh dear, now we have landed in the shit right up to our hooters. Excuse me, I'd better go and check with the Skipper. Slap his wrists sort of thing and try to bring him out of his alcoholic stupor.' He made a last attempt at humour and then he was gone – *quickly.*

Now as the Condor came lower and lower, the sun vanished behind them over the sparkling water and the fog thickened perceptibly. In an instant, or so it seemed to a frightened von Arco, it was blocking out all vision from the porthole at his side. The cabin became darker and darker. Now the lights on the massive control panel up front, where the two pilots hunched over their controls, glittered brightly in the sudden gloom.

The steward came up. Now his voice was no longer so gentle and friendly. Von Arco thought he detected a note of fear in it, too, when he spoke. 'Sir, if – er – anything happens, bring your feet up off the deck, lower your head and protect your face with your arms – like this.'

Von Arco gasped. 'Do you mean–'

'I mean nothing, sir. Just routine landing drill in – er – hazardous conditions.' And with that he was gone, too, to lie on the floor at the back of the plane, feet firmly wedged against a pile of heavy packing cases, hands over his eyes like some scared child trying to blot out a nightmare.

'Oh my God!' von Arco quavered as he glimpsed a hilltop through the fog, with pines marching up it like spike-helmeted Prussian guardsmen. 'We're going to hit the ground.'

'Hold on to your hat back there!' the young second pilot cried fervently without taking his eyes off the controls. *This is it!*

There was an ear-splitting roar as the pilot throttled back. The whole gigantic plane quivered under the almost unbearable strain. Behind an ashen-faced von Arco, the steward started to cry out the Act of Contrition at the top of his voice, as if he wanted to be sure that God heard him above all this racket.

The plane slammed to the ground. There was the whine of protesting rubber. Von Arco closed his eyes, white-knuckled hands desperately holding on to the seat in front of him. The plane lifted again – sickeningly. Again the engines roared. *Wham!* They were down for good now, the tyres howling shrilly. Von Arco risked a look. They were racing down a fog-shrouded runway at a tremendous speed. The firs were flashing by. He closed his eyes again quickly.

Suddenly, startlingly, it happened. The plane gave a sharp lurch. Something struck the port wing a tremendous blow. The Condor swung round. Von Arco felt the thud in his guts as it swung off the tarmac, completely out of control now. They bumped and jolted over rough ground, shredding pieces of the fuselage in a metallic wake behind them. With a great, grating metallic rending, the port wing was ripped off. The plane lurched and slithered violently. Was it ever going to stop its crazy progress across the fields? A tyre burst like an 88mm shell exploding. And then it appeared. Out of nowhere the hillside loomed up in the fog. There was nothing the two pilots could do now. They flung up their hands to protect their sweat-lathered fear-distorted faces.

C-R-U-M-P! At one hundred kilometres per hour, the stricken Condor smashed full tilt into the hillside. The undercarriage collapsed. The second pilot shrieked in mortal agony. Von Arco felt himself flung violently out of his seat. Something slammed against his temple and all went black.

Silence fell on the wrecked plane, the echoes dying away in those lonely hills. Thin shreds of cold grey fog began to embrace the dead Condor…

CHAPTER 4

'Gentlemen, *The President of the United States!*'

The assembled staff officers, secret servicemen and FBI agents rose to their feet at once and the chatter stopped as slowly the great doors opened and the President, supported by his son Elliott, crept slowly into the great stateroom.

For over twenty years now he had fought an endless battle against infantile paralysis; ever since that day back in 1921 when, having put out a forest fire up in Maine, he had gone for a swim in ice-cold water and had afterwards been seized by a deathly chill which had developed into the incurable disease. But he had not allowed himself to become a helpless invalid. He had fought his way to the highest office in the land and now the splendour of those two decades of effort shone in his calm, stone-carved face, as he lowered himself gratefully into a chair facing the company, placed a cigarette in his ivory cigarette-holder, lit it and said in that familiar, well-loved drawl, 'Gentlemen, please be seated.'

There was a shuffle of feet as the officers

and civilians sat down once more and waited.

Roosevelt gave them the full benefit of that massive profile, jaw jutting out doggedly, before he took the holder out of his mouth and said, 'Gentlemen, this is what I want to tell you. This day Mr Winston S. Churchill, the British Prime Minister, has sailed from Scotland,' he paused and delivered the punchline with the perfection and timing of one of his 'fireside chats', *to meet me!*'

Even the presence of the President could not quell the sudden outburst of excited chatter and Roosevelt smiled and winked happily at his big son. Elliott winked back.

'Now gentlemen, the reason I have called you here today is very simple. It is the question of security.' He looked at his own strapping Secret Service bodyguards. 'Not my own; you boys of the Secret Service look after me well enough. Why, Eleanor complains all the time you bozos won't even let her get near my bedroom to kiss me goodnight.' He laughed, throwing back his head so that it became almost a braying sound.

The others laughed with him, even Elliott, who knew his father had had nothing to do with his mother for years. He had other women for that.

'No, gentlemen, I am more worried about the security of my friend Mr Churchill. Do you know he walks around war-torn England guarded by only one detective, a certain Commander Thompson? Yes,' the President noted the looks of incredulity on his listeners' faces, 'you can believe me. One single detective! So gentlemen, it is going to be your – *our* – task to ensure that nothing happens to our – er – cousin from across the sea when he finally arrives here.' He looked at the big heavy-shouldered man with the greying hair in the front rank, who looked uneasy in civilian clothes, as if he were much more used to uniform. 'Chief Inspector MacKenzie of the Royal Canadian Mounted Police, you have something to say.'

One of the spectators whistled softly and said to his neighbour, 'So that's where it is gonna be – *Canada!*'

The Inspector stepped forward and snapped, 'Thank you, Mr President.' He turned to the others. 'In the Mounties, gentlemen, we learn to stand up, speak up and *shut up!*' The President's face cracked into a smile and some of the others laughed. MacKenzie was obviously a card. 'So I'll do exactly that. The Royal Canadian Mounted Police are going to run patrols right along the length of the Canadian eastern seaboard as far as the sixtieth parallel. The Royal Canadian Air Force is going to fly air patrol along the same route night and day to a depth of one hundred miles inland. So we feel that we've got the whole area tightly zipped up.' He looked at his audience with his hard, blue, suspicious policeman's eyes. 'The rest depends upon you, gentlemen,' he barked.

'What do you mean, Inspector?' An Army Air Corps Brigadier, smart in his pinks and elegantly cut tunic complete with Sam Browne, asked.

'This, Brigadier: we can clamp down on the press in Canada. There'll be no leaks on our side of the forty-ninth parallel. But can we be sure of you people below it?' He glared at the Americans, as if he didn't trust a single one of them.

There were stifled cries of outrage and someone murmured, 'Who in Sam Hill's name does that durn Canuck think he is?'

Hastily the President raised his hand for peace. 'Now, now, gentlemen,' he said, 'let us be fair! We all know about the calculated leak and how it does no harm for a fellah in politics if he gives the press boys a nice juicy tip-off.'

'Exactly, Mr President,' Mackenzie snapped. 'That's what we are afraid of north of the forty-ninth parallel, that someone in your *entourage*,' he emphasized the word, as if there was something obscene about it, 'might let slip to the press the details of your trip. I don't think it would take the Jerries long to put two and two together and figure out where you and Mr Churchill might possibly meet.'

Someone whistled softly and the Brigadier

in the Army Air Corps said hotly: 'But that's nonsense! The Krauts wouldn't dare to attack Churchill in the presence of the President. No sir!'

MacKenzie looked at Roosevelt, broad, tough cop's face blank of any emotion. Roosevelt responded immediately. 'I wonder ... I wonder, General Armstrong. What better way to show the Nazis' strength and Britain's weakness than to take out Mr Churchill in my presence? No, gentlemen, we must not underrate the Nazis' deviousness and sense of evil purpose.' The President stared around the assembly, while Inspector MacKenzie nodded his greying head in agreement. 'Gentlemen, it will be your task to ensure that nothing of that kind happens to our future comrade-in-arms. *Mr Winston S. Churchill must not die on the soil or in the waters of the North American continent...!*'

But if President Roosevelt was greatly concerned about the safety of his fellow leader, Churchill had other more mundane matters on his mind now that the great battleship had left sight of land and was plunging into the first of the gales which would plague her crossing. Now he squatted in the Admiral's sea cabin, clad in what he called the 'Teddy Suit', a blue woollen suit which zipped from neck to waist, old-fashioned spectacles poised at the end of his nose so that he looked a little like Mr Pickwick, frowning hard at the list in front of him. 'I have decided,' he declared grandly, 'we must feed the Former Naval Person something un-usual, seasonal and very definitely British, Purser. So it must be grouse.' He looked up at the attentive officer. 'Got it?'

'Yessir,' he answered. 'It was very nip-and-tuck. The shooting season only started on the first of August, but we had it rushed from Perth.'

'Excellent,' Churchill said and stared at the list once more. 'Now I have discovered that it was once the custom of the Lords of Admir-alty when they voyaged abroad to take with them a turtle, which they were entitled to draw from a naval establishment.' The purser began to look worried. 'This strange custom, it may interest you to know, started when Britain, in order to watch Napoleon at St Helena, took over Ascension Island and every warship returning home brought back with it a turtle. The custom has long since lapsed. However, I wish that the Former Naval Per-son, who himself was once the US Secretary of the Navy – hence his code-name – should see that the Royal Navy does not forget its ancient traditions.' He looked up at the purser, a cheeky grin on his moonlike face. 'I don't suppose you've got the odd couple of turtles aboard the *Prince of Wales*, have you?'

'No, sir. But, sir,' the flustered officer said

hastily, 'we *do* have some bottles of turtle soup left over from our commissioning dinner.'

Churchill beamed. 'Well, that's it then.' He pulled down his Royal Yacht Squadron waistcoat from the peg and held it up for the purser's inspection. 'I shall wear this, Purser. Do you think it will be appropriate?'

'Yessir. Very fitting, sir,' the officer replied, glad to have got safely through the preparations for the lunch that Churchill would give for Roosevelt.

Over the tannoy system a bugle started to sound. Churchill forgot the waistcoat. He glanced at his watch and said, 'Eleven o'clock. Pray, why are they sounding the bugle now, Purser?'

'It's "Up Spirits", sir. Still carried out at eleven sharp, even in wartime.'

Churchill beamed. 'Come, we shall watch,' he commanded, and zipping his 'Teddy' more tightly around the neck, he rose. Hastily the Purser sprang to his feet and opened the door for the Prime Minister.

For a while Churchill watched as the long line of mess orderlies jostled and pushed as they waited in line with their tins and pannikins, in front of the great oak cask bearing the legend *'The King, God Bless Him'*, for their share of the daily issue of rum and water; then he grew bored. 'What else have you to entertain me?' he demanded.

The Purser flashed a glance at his watch. '"Captain's Requestmen" has just started, sir,' he said.

'"Captain's Requestmen"?'

'Equivalent of the CO's orderly room in the Army, sir. The matelots – er, ratings, see an officer and put in their requests, sir.'

'Good, I will see it.'

Obediently the grinning sailors let themselves be pushed to one side as the Prime Minister, preceded by the Purser, set off for another entertainment, while the great battleship took another plunge into the waves in its slow, deliberate way.

Rows of ratings stood with their caps on in front of an officer in the Marine Barracks, a large open space on one of the lower decks. One by one they stepped forward and doffed their caps while they made their requests.

'Mostly, sir,' the Purser whispered in an intrigued Churchill's ear, 'they request allowances to be transferred from mothers to wives, that sort of thing. Pretty routine. But now and again you'll get a funny one. There might be one today if we're lucky.'

'Permission to grow, sir?' yet another rating was saying.

'What does that mean?' Churchill asked, puzzled even more when the officer replied, 'Permission to grow granted.'

'Permission to grow a beard, sir,' the Purser whispered. 'No beard may be grown in the

Royal Navy without the captain's permission. It's to prevent sailors from just being lazy and not shaving. Once permission has been granted, the rating cannot use a razor without official permission for three months.'

Churchill beamed. 'Another good old custom, rather like my turtles, eh?'

'Yes, like your turtles, sir,' the Purser echoed dutifully, wishing the Prime Minister would go away and let him get on with his own business.

A grizzled old man who must have been at least fifty now marched up to the officer, pulled off his cap and waited impatiently as the Coxswain bellowed out his name and rank: 'Able Seaman Thomas, sir!'

'Thomas is a character, sir,' the Purser whispered, suppressing a grin. 'A three-badge able seaman; we call them stripeys, sir. He hasn't much ambition, but he knows all the tricks of the trade.'

'Old,' Churchill agreed, 'but invaluable in wartime, I am sure, to balance the younger, inexperienced seamen.'

'Exactly, sir.'

Thomas saluted and focused his gaze on the bulkhead somewhere behind the officer's left shoulder. ''E pinched the end off 'n me banger, sir,' the old seaman said in an aggrieved voice, trying hard to suppress his indignation.

'Did what?' Churchill grinned.

'Pinched the end of me banger, sir,' Thomas repeated, not shifting his sphinx-like gaze. 'Ordinary Seaman 'awkins did.'

'Banger – what is that?' Churchill whispered.

'Sausage, sir. The other seaman must have stolen it.'

'Don't go much on Purser's sausages, sir,' Thomas went on. 'So I bought some NAAFI bangers – sausages, sir – and arranged with the cooks to burst the skins so that the ends stick out. I'm partial to 'em that way. I just turns me back for a minute to talk to a ship-mate when 'awkins nicks me ends. Nipped right orf, sir, and them's the best part.'

The officer sighed. 'So what am I supposed to do about it, Thomas?'

'I wants me revenge, sir. I wants permission to have a grudge fight, sir.'

The sorely tried officer looked at the Coxswain. 'Ordinary Seaman Hawkins will fight, sir,' he snapped.

'All right then,' the officer decided. 'Request granted. Fifteen hundred hours tomorrow on the upper deck.'

'Thank you, sir,' Thomas said and suddenly he grinned. 'I'll learn the young bastard,' he growled and then he was gone.

The Purser shook his head. 'Young Hawkins will slaughter Thomas. He's half Thomas's age and in top form, sir.'

Churchill smiled softly, as he turned away

and began to make his way back to the Admiral's sea cabin. 'It's perhaps not the age the counts, Purser,' he said deliberately, as if the little interchange had some special, private significance for him, *it is the spirit!*' He sighed heavily and for the first time the Purser realized just how old he was. Churchill had to be at least seventy and yet here he was, setting out on a dangerous voyage, completely unescorted, across the Atlantic, in a desperate attempt to gain America's support for his lone war against Hitler. Like old Stripey Thomas, who knew all the odds were stacked against him, he would go on fighting till the end. Abruptly Churchill's sudden sombre mood vanished. 'Just one more thing before you go, Purser.'

'Sir?'

'You can announce to the wardroom the film I have picked for tonight's performance after dinner.'

Hastily the Purser pulled out his notebook and pencil. 'Yessir. What is the title?'

Suddenly Churchill grinned mischievously. 'I thought we'd have a comedy for a change. What about Laurel and Hardy in,' he hesitated only a second, 'in *Saps at Sea*. Now don't you think that is a highly appropriate title?' Without waiting for an answer, he waddled away...

CHAPTER 5

Christian eyed the shore without pleasure. It was a desolate scene that presented itself as the camouflaged U-69 limped along the shore of Canada. He saw a wavering coastline of deserted little beaches and coves, shrouded in a thin grey mist, behind which the empty countryside rose into mournful hills, covered in dense woods of fir and birch.

'Looks like something out of Karl May, sir,' Frenssen observed.

'Didn't know you could read, Frenssen,' Christian answered, telling himself that the big *Obermaat* was right. There were the same lonely estuaries and thick woods of the 19th century writer's tales, and one half expected to spot some lurking Indian or leather-clad trapper paddling his birch-bark canoe. But there was not a living soul as far as the eye could see, not one human dwelling, not one spiral of smoke from house or camp fire. Nothing but primeval hills and the cold grey sea.

'Anyway, we can thank God for the fog,' Christian said, taking his gaze off that bleak, inhospitable coastline. 'It'll give us a little bit of cover and we certainly need it here.'

'I agree, sir,' Frenssen answered, casting a swift look at the sky. 'Feel very naked out here, like the proverbial wet fart waiting to hit the side of the thunderbox.'

'Something like that.' For some time now, he knew, the operators below had been receiving feeble radar impulses from various sources, but whether they were from enemy aircraft, the operators were unable to make out. 'Well, if all goes according to plan, Frenssen, we should be making contact with this mysterious guide of ours soon.'

'Better be really soon,' Frenssen said, wiping the damp spray from his brick-red face with his paw, 'because our diesel isn't going to last much longer and I wouldn't trust the electric motors anymore. If we go down with them, I'm thinking, sir, we might well stay down – for good!'

'Yes,' Christian agreed grimly, 'as you would phrase it in your delightful manner, Frenssen, "we've really got our eggs caught in a rat-trap this time." We're running out of diesel and–'

'Sir!' the forward lookout's voice cut urgently into his words. 'Aircraft, bearing one-two-five... Distance five hundred ... *approaching!*'

Christian whipped up his glasses, while Frenssen flung himself behind the conning tower's machine-gun. Two fat-bellied white shapes zoomed into the circles of gleaming calibrated glass. 'Hudsons!' Christian cried out, identifying them immediately.

'Shit, now the clock is really in the pisspot!' Frenssen snapped back the loading handle and prepared to blast them out of the sky.

'Don't fire!' Christian yelled urgently as the roar of the plane engines grew louder by the instant. 'Even if we did knock them out of the sky, there'd be more, and we haven't a chance here. Pray that the camouflage – and the fog – fools them.'

'Christ on a crutch, that's a frigging pious hope if there ever was one,' Frenssen growled sullenly. Reluctantly he took his hands off the gun.

Mind racing electrically, his breath coming in short sharp gasps, Christian watched as the planes started to come lower. The one to the right waggled its wings suddenly. Christian's heart skipped a beat. That meant he had been spotted. He braced himself. Would their camouflage fool the enemy? With a sudden sinking feeling he knew it wouldn't – *it simply couldn't!*

Now the two planes were less than a couple of hundred metres away winging down over the water, patched here and there with the writhing grey mist, coming in very fast.

Suddenly there was a sharp dry crack. Christian, watching mesmerized, jumped. Bright red flame showered from the sky. The fog glared like a sheet of flame. 'They're dropping parachute flares, sir!' Frenssen yelled. 'They've rumbled us, sir!'

'Let 'em have it!' Christian cried, knowing that they hadn't a chance, but telling himself that he was going to go down fighting. Frenssen pressed the trigger of the machine-gun. Tracer zipped up, shredding the fog with its white-burning ferocity. The leading Hudson banked sharply to starboard, put off by the sudden burst of fire. Christian yelled down the voice-pipe, 'Frahm, let me have all you can get out of that diesel—'

The first bomb exploded with a tremendous roar fifty metres away. The U-69 rocked madly, as if struck by a sudden tornado. A great shower of cold water splashed over the bridge. Christian gasped with the shock of it. But Frenssen, drenched as he was stuck grimly to his gun, swinging it round as if it were a toy, and peppered the sky in front of the second Hudson.

But the pilot was not to be put off. The plane came in low, winging over the water at a tremendous speed, dragging its great black shadow behind it over the low fog. Christian knew exactly what the pilot would do: as soon as he got within bombing distance, he would soar straight into the sky and drop his deadly eggs.

Frenssen knew the tactic too. Now he stopped firing and raised his machine-gun, waiting for that moment when the Hudson would expose its naked belly. Then he would strike.

At that moment the white-painted bomber seemed to fill the whole sky. Christian could see every detail, from the red, white and blue emblem painted on its wings to the pale faces of the pilots behind the gleaming Perspex canopy, so sure that this time they wouldn't miss. The roar was ear-splitting. Below, the surface of the sea raged and foamed in the plane's prop-wash.

'*Now!*' Christian screamed, as the pilot suddenly jerked back the stick and the Hudson shot upwards. Frenssen grunted harshly. He pressed the trigger. At 1,000 rounds per minute the bullets streaked upwards.

Suddenly Christian could see quite clearly the metal fabric of the plane being ripped and shredded mercilessly. Almost at once thick, black oily smoke started to pour from the Hudson's port engine. Still it continued to climb, shedding a metallic rain behind as Frenssen's tracer ripped and tore at the length of the plane's belly.

'*Watch out!*' one of the lookouts on the foredeck shouted urgently. '*The whoreson is shitting on us!*' He flung himself flat on the deck as the stick of bombs hurtled downwards.

'*One ... two ... three ... four...!* Four savage eruptions heaved the U-69 out of the water, as if it were a child's toy. It slammed down again the next instant in a great plume of whirling white spray. Seawater shot upwards in crazy geysers as the diesel stopped then started a moment later; but in that same instant the rudder jammed and the U-69 started to swerve in an arc.

'*Verdammte Scheisse!*' Christian cried, enraged, and slammed his fist against the bulkhead, as the second Hudson, now trailing black smoke behind it, began to streak for the land. 'Now this!'

'Here comes the first one again!' the deck-hand sang out, clambering to his feet.

'Take this, Tommy!' Frenssen hissed through gritted teeth and pressed his trigger. Swinging the gun from side to side, he flung up a wall of flying white tracer in the path of the Hudson.

But the pilot must have been a veteran. He flung the big two-engined bomber from left to right and then back again to dodge the fire, as if he were flying some nimble little fighter. Time and time again Frenssen missed hitting him by a hair's breadth. And now he was coming in for the kill, streaking across the surface of the sea and whipping up the waves beneath him, while the U-69 curved helplessly. This time, Christian knew, with a feeling of utter despair, he simply could not miss. But the U-69 was not fated to die – *yet*.

In the very same instant that the Hudson began to rise steeply, blowing hot exhaust fumes over their upturned petrified faces, prior to dropping its bombs, the crippled U-boat was abruptly submerged in a clinging grey fog.

Immediately everything was changed. They were still drifting, admittedly, but the Hudson had lost its target in the thick fog which rolled down the sides of the U-69, muffling the sound of his one engine and muting the noise of the suddenly frustrated Hudson. 'Stop engine!' Christian hissed down the voice-pipe, as the Hudson's pilot might hear him.

Frahm reacted immediately. The throb of the diesel stopped at once. Now all was tense silence as the Hudson circled and circled somewhere above them, repeatedly dropping its flares, trying to find its intended victim. But that was not to be, and after a frustrated search the pilot gave up. Slowly but surely the drone of its engines died away and all was complete silence save for the mournful *drip-drip* of the wet fog.

Christian breathed a sigh of relief and wiped the sweat from his forehead, before ordering the engine to be started again, while at the bow, the lookouts strained desperately, peering through the fog. Behind Christian, Frenssen relaxed his grip on the gun and cocked his big head to one side.

'The Tommy's gone,' Christian reassured him.

'It's not that, sir. I can hear something out there.'

'What? The guide-boat's engine?'

'No. Sounds more like surf running!'

'Christ, not that too!' Christian moaned. Hastily he dropped down the conning tower ladder onto the deck and ran its length to where the lookouts were poised, heads cocked to one side, too. 'Can you hear anything?' he snapped.

'Yessir,' the bigger of the two answered. 'Surf– *Look!*'

Suddenly the fog parted and Christian caught a glimpse of ugly black rocks, washed with foam, directly to the U-69's front. They had been caught in a current, which would soon dash them onto the rocks, where their hull would be apart. He cupped his hands to his mouth. 'Frenssen – quick!' he bellowed. 'Tell the Chief ... one hundred and twenty revolutions to the port shaft! If he doesn't make it quick, we'll crash into the cliffs. *Los, Mensch!*'

'One hundred and twenty port shaft!' Frenssen yelled into the voice-tube. Nothing happened.

Desperately Christian shrieked, 'Frenssen, tell the chief: another fifty– *Quick!*'

'He can't take the responsibility!' Frenssen hollered back, face streaming with spray from the pounding waves. 'The engine's gonna bust!'

'*Fuck the engine!* We'll all go bust in a minute!' Christian screamed at him as the U-69 crept ever closer to the rocks, their black, craggy contours sprayed and splattered by the angry white water. 'Two hundred and make it fast. *Dalli … dalli!*'

The U-69 shivered like a live thing as the vibrations increased with a grating howl and the screws thrashed the water in fury, the plates groaning in protest. With agonizing slowness, while Christian felt his heart thumping at such a crazy rate that it seemed it might burst out of his ribcage at any moment, the battered submarine edged its way out of the trap. Twice the waves reached out and tugged at the U-69, as if they wanted to drag her onto those threatening rocks, and twice the lone diesel, throbbing all-out, fought them off, leaving them to retreat, hissing sullenly, cheated of their prey. And then they were round the cove, the rocks disappearing behind them in the mist, the U-69 steering a crazy course, but freed from the danger at last, heading straight for the little fishing boat which had appeared from nowhere.

Christian slumped, all energy spent, against the base of the conning tower, not even possessing enough strength to assess whether the strange boat meant new danger or not.

Slowly it chugged closer and closer…

CHAPTER 6

Doktor Ritter (if that was really his name) cleared his throat angrily as he eyed the smouldering wreck of the crashed Condor. 'You have done a very foolish thing, *Kapitänleutnant* von Arco!' he snapped in an accented German which bore witness to the many years he had spent in the service of the *Abwehr* in North America. Obviously by now he was more used to speaking American.

Von Arco flushed, but kept back the angry reply which had immediately flown to his lips. Out here in this Godforsaken wilderness he needed this little man, with his check shirt, laced boots and revolver slung from his hip so that he looked like some comic cowboy from a Hans Albers film. 'I thought it was standard operating procedure when a plane goes down, to destroy it, *Herr Doktor*,' he answered, wiping the sweat off his dirty face, while behind him the *Luftwaffe* survivors erected two cairns of stones over the shallow graves they had dug for the dead pilots.

'It might be in Europe, but not here, von Arco. The plane wreckage my people from German Bay could have cleared away, but the scorched grass and gorse now that you have set fire to the damn thing will last for ages.' He snapped his fingers angrily as if he were mentally dismissing the matter. 'Well, mustn't cry over spilled milk. I'll see what I can do about the damned thing later. Let me get your people and yourself into German Bay as soon as possible. And for God's sake, why did they kit you out in that damned uniform? You stick out like a sore thumb in it!'

Von Arco flushed even more. But he restrained himself with difficulty. 'Sorry,' he forced himself to say humbly, though inside he was raging. He promised himself that once he had returned to the Reich he would settle the arrogant little bastard's hash for him, even if he had to go as high as Father Christmas himself.

'All right, into the truck, the lot of you,' Ritter commanded, 'and you fly-boys, don't bother about those graves any more. As soon as I get my people from German Bay up here, those are the first things they will clear away. With a bit of luck before this day is over, we're going to make sure that there is not a piece of evidence left that you were ever here. Now – *move it!*' he barked and it was obvious from his tone that the little man in his too-large Stetson and check shirt was used to having his orders obeyed – immediately. Von Arco moved instinctively to the cab, where the driver, a long, lean individual similarly clad to Ritter waited, his jaws moving steadily back and forth as he chewed on the wad of tobacco that bulged from the side of his mouth. Ritter stopped him. 'In the back with the rest, von Arco,' he barked, 'and get under the canvas until I tell you to come out. I am not taking a single chance on this one. Now let's get the show on the road...!'

Thus it was that von Arco found himself half an hour later bumping down a rutted dirt road into the little waterside settlement, getting his first glimpse of German Bay from under a sheet of stinking canvas.

German Bay was a handful of wooden shanties hanging on to the foot of the cliff, centred on a small church, also of wood, painted a hideous blue. The air was full of the stink of fish and von Arco soon saw why. From the jetties that led from the house straight down to the cove, everywhere there was cod hanging up to dry in the weak sun. Here and there he spotted from his hiding place lean, tough-looking men, wearing check shirts and splashing through the mud of the main street in high laced boots.

'What a one-horse town, sir,' the steward, who crouched next to him, whispered. 'If this is the land of unlimited possibilities, give me old Munich any time.' And von Arco was forced to agree with the Bavarian. The place really was the arsehole of the world.

A moment or two later, the ancient Ford truck shuddered to a stop and the driver's hard hand slapped the canvas. 'All out,' he called in a German that was barely recognisable as such. Von Arco stumbled down into the muddy lane with the others, his nostrils assailed even more strongly by the stink of the decaying cod from which the locals extracted cod liver oil, to find they had left German Bay up the cliff behind them.

Now they were on the edge of the bay itself, surrounded by melancholy countryside, dotted with dwarf firs and with mudbrown streams gurgling and bubbling their way through peaty soil into the placid grey water. A little bewildered, they stood there, wondering why they had been brought here instead of to the village, but not for long.

Abruptly Doktor Ritter appeared from the ground, with only his head showing so that he would have appeared ludicrous in any other circumstances but these, and snapped in that harsh incisive manner of his, 'Over here, von Arco – and the rest of you, too. *Los!*'

Obediently they ran across the lumpy, boggy ground like a bunch of raw recruits and stared down at the hole, which proved to be man-made, its sides carefully constructed of concrete, with an iron ladder fixed to it leading down to the brightly-lit interior below. Von Arco gasped with surprise. After what he had just seen in German Bay, he had not expected this sort of thing.

Ritter chuckled. 'Yes, you thought you had

landed in the arsehole of the world, didn't you? And in a way you are right; German Bay *is* that celebrated orifice. But it provides just the right cover we need. Here you will see what we have done with that cover over the last few months. Follow me and watch your step. The rungs are a little slick.' With that he disappeared down the ladder with surprising speed for a man of his age, followed a little more hesitantly by the others…

'We modelled it on the U-boat pens at Lorient,' Ritter explained, his voice echoing hollowly in the great cave that stretched as far as the eye could see. The water lapping its length gently was oil-scummed, clear evidence that there had been ships inside the great cave at some time or other. 'But of course, this is far better than Lorient. After all, Germans built it, not the decadent frogs.' He looked at von Arco mockingly and the latter could not help thinking that somehow or other, the little agent was pulling his leg.

Von Arco stared in wonder at this engineering marvel in the middle of nowhere. There were twelve pens which could be used as dry docks, each one separated from its neighbour by a massive concrete partition, and the entrance from the bay to each pen could be concealed by lowering a massive steel shutter. By the side of each pen there was heaped the latest equipment needed to repair and service a U-boat: oxyacetylene burners, cranes, special cradles for supporting torpedoes, all the old familiar apparatus he remembered from Murwik in Germany somehow transported here. Ritter seemed to be able to read a bewildered von Arco's mind, for he said, 'Transport subs. We've been running them from Brest and Lorient for months now, ever since we decided that this place would make more than just a secret met station. We even imported specialised workers.' He pointed towards the end of the massive underground chamber, from whence warm yellow lights glowed. 'Pattern shops, smithies, machine shops, torpedo and periscope workshops – the whole works.' He smiled. 'Everything a good submariner's heart could desire and all manned by the cheapest and most reliable labour thinkable.'

Von Arco looked at him. 'Not the locals?' he asked.

'Of course not. Good Germans they might be, but skilled industrial workers they are not. No, my dear von Arco, our labour comes to us courtesy of Uncle Joe.'

'*Uncle Joe?*'

'Yes, that's what we here in North America call the Russian leader Josef Stalin.'

'Russians?'

'Exactly. Russian submarine specialists, captured in June in their bases in Eastern Poland. Your chief, Admiral Doenitz,

offered them a choice. Work for us or else...'
He left the rest of the sentence unsaid.

Von Arco nodded his understanding, as Ritter hitched up the pistol at his hip more comfortably. 'Well, *Herr Kapitänleutnant,* this then is your new headquarters.' Ritter extended his hand like a head waiter welcoming a prosperous customer into a restaurant and gave a mock bow. 'Please take over, while I collect some of my chaps from German Bay and attempt to clear up the mess you left up at the site of the crash. Good day!' With that he was gone, clambering up the ladder like a plump monkey in cowboy dress, leaving von Arco and the equally bewildered *Luftwaffe* men staring at their new surroundings.

Slowly von Arco circled the pens, stepping over the rubber-sheathed cables which were everywhere, staring at them thoughtfully, telling himself they would easily house the survivors of the wolf packs, which were due to arrive in the bay within the next twenty-four hours. After that he would have a mere forty hours to assign them to their new patrol areas between grid square AI94 and BB90. Once one of the wolf packs had spotted the President's ship, he would order them all to converge and attack by pack. Suddenly his apprehension at being in this remote place, stranded without any means of return – and he'd no doubts about what'd happen once the balloon went up: the enraged English would wipe it off the face of the map – vanished. He'd found a solution to his problem.

His arrogant, vain face lit up under the grime and smoke stains, as he stared at the entrance to the great cave. Of course, he had it! Not only would he be the officer who had conceived and directed the operation to kill that drunken sot Churchill, but now he had found a way to save himself and enjoy the honours that the Führer would undoubtedly shower upon him. *One of the wolf packs would not sail with the rest! It would be kept behind!* He'd find some excuse to detain it. After all, all the Big Lion's authority was invested in him. He could do what he liked in German Bay. As soon as whoever sunk the *Prince of Wales* reported his kill, he would order the submarine that stayed behind to sail immediately – with himself on board. Perhaps they'd use grid square AI94, well away from the enraged surface craft looking for the U-boat which had sunk the pride of the Royal Navy. Undoubtedly the captain of the submarine which stayed behind would complain and bitch. But by the time they got back to the Reich and discovered what had been the fate of the rest of the wolf packs, he would undoubtedly change his mind, especially if he, von Arco, recommended him for a decoration. The German Cross in Gold, perhaps, nothing too spectacular.

Von Arco smiled happily at his reflection

in the oil-scummed water. Yes, he told himself, it was all going to work out after all.

'Sir,' the voice of one of the *Luftwaffe* men cut into his happy reverie.

He spun round to where the little group of survivors stood. 'What is it?' he demanded.

'There's something coming in through the entrance.'

Von Arco stared in the direction the speaker was indicating and caught the first glimpse of the mutilated submarine limping into the cave, its side holed and dented, streaked with patches of red lead resembling the symptoms of some loathsome skin disease, bringing with it that typical stench of a U-boat returning from a long patrol: a mixture of rust, oil, stale acid, burnt rubber, seawater, human sweat – *and fear.* He screwed up his eyes in the yellow gloom to catch sight of the numerals painted on her conning tower which would indicate what craft she was. But that coarse Hamburg waterfront voice bellowing away happily, *'Onwards, onwards, through the heavens pouring with piss. Send me back to Murwik cos it can't be frigging worse than this,'* told him all he wanted to know.

'Frenssen,' he said. '*Obermaat* Frenssen!'

Next moment he saw the number on the battered, shell-pocked turret and he knew he had the U-boat which would take him back safely to Germany when it was all over – the *U-69...*

BOOK THREE

Operation Death Watch

'Von Arco's gonna use the U-69 for a quick bunk back to the Homeland, that's his game, mark my frigging words!'

Obermaat Frenssen to Christian Jungblut

CHAPTER 1

Inspector MacKenzie frowned at his paper-littered desk and then at the racket coming from outside. Down below in the street French-Canadians were protesting against Canada introducing conscription once again. *'Pas de service militaire!'* they were chanting as they marched up and down in front of the City Hall, watched by a couple of bored Mounties. *'No conscription... Pas de...'*

Irritated by their constant shouting and the problems he was facing this hot August day, he barked, 'Lejoly, willye shut that bluidy window. I can't hear myself think for yon frogs and their blether!'

Sub-Inspector Lejoly, a French-speaking Mountie himself, from Quebec, grinned. He knew that the dour old Scot's bark was worse than his bite. Besides, this job of being responsible for Churchill's safety was an awesome burden for MacKenzie. Obediently he rose and slammed the window closed, remarking: 'What's wrong with those goddam frog-eaters? You'd think they'd be only too glad to go to Europe and have their stupid frog heads blown off for King

161

Georgie.' He grinned at his boss.

MacKenzie returned his grin in a weary kind of a way. 'Ay, I suppose you're right, Lejoly. Protestant Canada hasn't treated you French-Canadians too well all these years. But ye ken, Lejoly, they would be fighting for *France* as well.'

Lejoly shrugged and dismissed the matter. 'One day they'll fight too, sir. Now, sir, the US press has blown the whistle on President Roosevelt. They're stating openly in today's editions that when the President sails on his summer vacation cruise, he will go to meet Churchill.'

'Ay,' MacKenzie snorted. 'And poor old Churchill's been at sea since Monday without any escort whatsoever.' He consulted his calendar. 'It will be Wednesday, August 6th before the *Prince of Wales* receives a destroyer escort from the Royal Canadian Navy sailing out of Iceland.' He reached out and took another stiff slug of scotch from the glass in front of him.

Lejoly gave a little sigh. It was only ten in the morning and the chief was already well into a fifth of the stuff. But still, he consoled himself, MacKenzie was reputed to have a head as hard as the granite from his native Aberdeen. 'Naval authorities state, sir, that there is no chance of any German surface vessel being able to stop the *Prince of Wales*,' he said.

'It's no them surface vessels I'm worrying about, laddie,' MacKenzie said grimly, slapping the report in front of him with his knuckles. 'Look at this. Two of our Hudsons attacked a surfaced U-boat, camouflaged as a cargo vessel, right in the entrance to bluidy Placentia Bay itself. Then this!' He rapped the desk angrily once more. 'Although we know from British Naval Intelligence in London that there are at least three wolf packs at sea in the North Atlantic, there has not been a single attack on any of our convoys for the last forty-eight hours and during that period of time the U-boats have maintained perfect radio silence. Our code experts have picked up nair a word. Now what do you make of that, Lejoly?'

The dark-haired French-Canadian pursed his lips. 'It almost looks, sir,' he said slowly, trying to ignore the muted chant from outside, 'as if something is on... As if the U-boats might be concentrating for an attack–'

'An attack on the bluidy *Prince of Wales!*' MacKenzie exploded. 'An attack on poor old Mr Churchill!'

'Exactly, sir. But the North Atlantic is a very big place, and we of the Royal Mounted Police are land-based.'

MacKenzie did not seem to hear the comment. Instead he said, 'Ye ken, I know the Old Man, Lejoly.'

'Churchill?'

'Ay, I was with him in the trenches in France in Sixteen. He was our battalion commander and a grand one at that and all. They'd kicked him out of the cabinet in disgrace and I mind that he'd have liked to die with all the other good lads who died in Flanders that winter.' MacKenzie took a long thoughtful drink of his whisky and Lejoly told himself that beneath that dour, craggy Scots exterior there was an emotional man, a sentimentalist. 'So ye see, Lejoly, I've always had a bit of personal interest in Mr Churchill. Ay, that I have.' Suddenly his voice rose and he was very businesslike again. 'Now, Lejoly, I think we agree that there's something in the wind. The Huns are gonna have a crack at the PM?' Lejoly nodded his agreement. 'We're agreed as well that they're going to do it with their damned U-boats.' Again Lejoly nodded. 'Now those fly-boys who attacked that lone U-boat in the Hudsons reported that it did not attempt to dive when attacked, which is their standard operating procedure. Remember, too, that the damned thing was camouflaged as a cargo vessel. So what do you make o' that?' he rasped almost aggressively.

Lejoly did not hesitate. 'She'd been hit, sir. She was limping along on the surface, camouflaged because she could not dive.'

'Exactly. But where in the devil's name was she going to?' MacKenzie snorted angrily. 'I dinna ken, Lejoly. But I'll bet ye a dollar to a dime that if we can find yon lone U-boat, we'll find the rest of yon murdering buggers.'

'Do you mean, sir, that you think the Nazis have got a hiding place off the coast of Canada?' Lejoly exclaimed, puffing out his cheeks in that gallic fashion of his.

'I do, Lejoly, and we've got to damnwell find it – and find it soon, before Churchill arrives here – or else...' He left the rest of his words unsaid, but Lejoly knew well what he meant. Suddenly he felt an icy finger of fear trace its way down the small of his back and he shivered.

Inspector Thompson, Churchill's faithful bodyguard for nearly twenty years, shivered too in the icy wind that blew from the Atlantic, as the great rehearsal got underway. 'Will you just look at him,' he snarled out of the side of his mouth to the Purser. 'Fancy standing in this wind without his bloody overcoat. He'll get his death of cold!'

The Purser stared at Churchill, who was wearing only a yachting cap and a navy blue suit, as he stood on the deck in the stiff wind supervising the rehearsal for his ceremonial meeting with the President. 'Don't mention death – of any kind, Inspector,' he whispered. 'There are enough buzzes about Mr Churchill and death going around the ship as it is.'

'Buzzes, what kind of buzzes?' Thompson demanded in that suspicious policeman's manner of his, his master forgotten for a moment.

'Oh, that the Jerries are sending a surface craft to intercept us before we can link up with our Canadian Navy escort... That they might try to bomb us with their long-range Focke Condors... Submarine, of course. The matelots have been rabbiting on for days now that there are Jerry U-boats waiting for us on the other side.'

Thompson pondered the information while across the deck the Royal Marine Band began to play as Churchill walked up and shook the hand of the official playing the role of Roosevelt, followed by the Chiefs-of-Staff, who did the same. Now the ship's officers began to advance in single file, giving an 'eyes right' to the man acting as President as they marched by.

'Don't like it,' Churchill barked suddenly. 'Some of you officers are not putting enough snap into it.' He grinned suddenly and took a quick puff at his big cigar. 'I shall have to re-introduce the lash. Make you jump. All right, Marines start up again and let's do it one more time.'

Thompson shook his head in mock wonder. 'Will you look at him, pushing seventy and standing out in the perishing cold as if he were a ruddy teenager. And all the time we could be torpedoed at any moment.'

The Purser forced a laugh. 'Between you and me, Inspector, I think there's nothing the PM would like better than a bit of action.'

'By the way, what happens to him if we go into action?' Thompson asked.

'He goes below the armour plate.'

Thompson frowned. 'Well, that might be the rule, Purser, but I wouldn't like to be the man who ordered him to go down there. I know him of old, and I know where *he* would want to be in action.'

'And where's that, Inspector?'

'*On the damned bridge, of course, in the ruddy thick of it!*'

The rehearsal was over at last. Now the Prime Minister went down to the Map Room, which was a replica in miniature of his old Map Room at the Admiralty when he had been First Sea Lord. One wall was taken up by an enormous map of the Atlantic Ocean. It was lit by strip lighting and on it the position of every ship, warship and merchantman was marked, plus the position of every German U-boat, by sinister little coffin-shaped ebony pins.

Quietly puffing his cigar, while busy naval officers moved back and forth bringing new information to be placed on the map, he stared at it, his Chiefs-of-Staff grouped behind him. 'Does it not seem strange to you, Captain Pym,' he asked the grey-haired naval officer in charge of the map, 'that although there is a very large convoy proceeding eastwards,' he indicated the sixty or seventy red ships which were merchantmen, surrounded by grey ships which signified warships, 'there are no U-boats in their path? Indeed, is it not of some significance that according to your map, the whole Nazi U-boat fleet seems to be concentrated in the *South* Atlantic with none at all in the North?'

Veteran that he was, the grey-haired naval officer flushed and for a moment seemed at a loss for words. Then he said, 'The fact has not escaped us, sir. Naval Intelligence in London has been working on the enemy U-boat radio traffic for the last seventy-two hours, night and day, non-stop. But there is nothing, absolutely nothing on the air concerning the North Atlantic.' He frowned heavily. 'Try as they may, nothing turns up.'

Now it was Churchill's turn to frown. He liked problems solved – and solved quickly.

A junior officer came in and whispered hurriedly into Captain Pym's ear. He smiled and cleared his throat noisily. 'I have the pleasure to inform you, sir, that we have just heard that an enemy U-boat has been sunk off the Azores – there, sir,' he indicated the spot on the map and, removing the black coffin pin, threw it into a tray.

Churchill's frown vanished. His pudgy, moonlike face creased into a smile. 'Excellent, Pym, excellent. But let me say this to you. Only British submarines are *sunk*. German U-boats are *destroyed*, mark that, please.'

'Yessir.'

The problem of the apparent lack of enemy submarines in the North Atlantic seemingly now forgotten, Churchill turned on his Chiefs-of-Staff and said, 'Gentlemen, I have an announcement to make. I have decided where I shall take council with the Former Naval Person. He and I have kept this secret even from our staffs for obvious security reasons, and we all know how our American cousins are virtually paranoid about security.'

Dill, big bluff and white-haired, the Chief of the Imperial General Staff, cleared his throat and barked, 'But very wise, very wise indeed, if I may say so.'

Churchill ignored the Field Marshal. He had always disdained elaborate security precautions. 'Gentlemen,' he growled in that familiar style of speaking which had thrilled millions of listeners these last terrible months, 'on Saturday 9th August, 1941, I shall meet President Roosevelt in the Bay of Placentia. If God so wills, it will be an historic meeting, one that may well decide the fate of western democracy.' He spun round and stabbed the big map with a pudgy forefinger. 'There, gentlemen, we will meet to symbolize the deep underlying unities which stir and, at decisive moments, rule the English-speaking peoples throughout the world.' He raised one finger, as if addressing a mass audience. 'Would it be presumptuous of me to say that it symbolizes something more majestic – namely, the marshalling of the good forces of the world against the evil forces which are now so formidable and triumphant, and have cast their cruel spell over the whole of Europe?' He stared at the map, eyes suddenly full of tears. 'Placentia,' he said gruffly, as if the name itself was of great significance, *'Placentia!'* Slowly a large tear began to roll down his cheek…

CHAPTER 2

The surviving skippers moved in single file along the concrete ramp, past the damaged submarines, for virtually every U-boat had undergone some sort of attack since they had sailed from Germany four weeks before. Indeed, all three wolf pack commanders had disappeared with their boats, leaving the U-boats now commanded by young, enthusiastic but relatively inexperienced officers.

Christian, bringing up the rear and trying to avoid stumbling over the tangles of cables and machine parts which were everywhere, flung a glance at the U-69. Now her belly gaped like a disembowelled whale, while the Russian specialists swarmed over her, cutting off large sections of her outer hull with their glaring-blue torches. He frowned. Why had von Arco ordered such extensive repairs, he wondered, when they were probably due to sail in a couple of days' time? Still, he told himself, the Russians worked a great deal harder than the average German dockie, and they worked in two shifts all round the clock. They had to! Their civilian guards from German Bay tolerated no slacking. Any Russian resting for even a minute soon felt the weight of the pick-axe handles they all carried. The men of German Bay were hard task-masters: they were not given to leniency.

They passed the U-44, its conning tower buckled and twisted grotesquely by an English bomb. In front of Christian, Kammhuber, its Skipper, grinned and said over his shoulder, 'Thought I'd bought the farm that time, Jungblut. Wow, what an explosion!'

Christian grinned. 'Yes, by rights you look as if you should have been playing the harp by now!'

They swung round a group of crewmen, mostly pale-faced kids in their late teens, too young even to grow the beards that the older men, unable to shave, grew while on a cruise. They were clustered around the shattered pressure hull of another U-boat, staring in awe in that fitful flickering light at the Russian workers tearing down the buckled plates, as if they couldn't believe they and the boat had survived such tremendous damage. Christian shook his head as he passed them. What a collection of greenbeaks they were! Whatever the operation was going to be, they would be damned hard-pressed to execute it successfully with these inexperienced crews.

But if Christian was doubtful about the success of whatever the Big Lion had

172

planned for them, *Kapitänleutnant* von Arco had no doubts whatsoever; he simply radiated confidence. '*Meine Herren*,' he barked in a fair imitation of the Big Lion's harsh, clipped style of speech, 'let me welcome you to Operation Death Watch!' He stared around the circle of pale, attentive faces as they sat there in the big concrete ops room, while in his turn Doktor Ritter stared at von Arco intently, as if he were seeing him for the very first time. 'Operation Death Watch!' Von Arco toyed with the words. 'At present the name means nothing to you, of course, or to anyone else except a close circle of high officers, and, naturally, the Führer,' he said the name of the leader as if it were in quotes, 'for, *meine Herren*, the Führer himself has sanctioned this great mission! So what is Operation Death Watch? I shall tell you.' He paused and straightened himself up to his full height. 'It is an operation designed not only to knock out the most powerful ship in the English fleet, but also to assassinate that arch English plutocrat – *Mr Winston Churchill!*'

There was a collective gasp of surprise, as if someone had just punched all of them in the stomach. 'Winston Churchill!' Kammhuber echoed, awe in his voice. 'Oh my, my, my, then the tick-tock will really be in the pisspot!' Silently Christian agreed with him.

But as von Arco smirked arrogantly,

pleased with the surprise he had sprung on them, *Doktor* Ritter's frown deepened. Suddenly, for reasons known only to himself, he looked like a sorely troubled man.

'Comrades,' von Arco continued. 'Churchill is to meet Roosevelt soon, somewhere off the eastern seaboard of the United States or Canada and it is our intention to show that Jew Roosevelt just how long and strong the arm of the German *Wehrmacht* is...' Swiftly and expertly von Arco sketched in the details of the bold dramatic plan, while they listened enthralled, hardly daring to believe their own ears and Doktor Ritter's worried look grew ever more intense. Christian, listening intently with the rest, trying to overcome his repugnance for von Arco for his past cowardice, felt a growing sense of disquiet as the plan unfolded. It was a proper and legitimate act of war to sink the *Prince of Wales*. After all, it was an enemy warship which only months before had taken part in the operations which had sent the pride of the *Kriegsmarine,* Germany's newest and greatest capital ship, the *Bismarck,* to the bottom of the Atlantic. But assassinating Churchill, a civilian, in cold blood was another thing altogether. Indeed, he had always had a sneaking regard for the Old Man, ever since he had replaced that bumbling, mealy-mouthed Chamberlain with his silly hat and even sillier umbrella. Now was he, Christian

Jungblut, going to be part of the operations which would kill the Englishman? But if he didn't like the plan, the faces of his fellow skippers showed only too clearly just how enthusiastic they were. Their eyes glowed and their lean, hard faces were set in expressions of fanatical eagerness, as if they could not get away soon enough to carry it out. They were like highly-strung greyhounds straining at the leash, waiting to be allowed onto the track.

'Heaven, arse and cloudburst!' Kammhuber cried exuberantly, when von Arco paused. 'The tin there'll be in this one for all of us! The factories that produce the Iron Cross will be working overtime after this!'

'Yes,' von Arco agreed, fingering his own Knight's Cross and telling himself that the glowing-faced young skipper would probably not survive the great operation, 'all of you will be able to cure your throatache this time.'

'Think of the gash and the champus afterwards!' Kammhuber cried, carried away by the thought of what rewards that coveted Knight's Cross would bring once they were back in the Reich, 'the beaver will be lining up at my bedside, just waiting to be parted by yours truly!' They all laughed uproariously and even von Arco allowed himself a careful smile.

Christian, however, was still worried and uncertain and for some reason, as the rest broke into excited chatter, his gaze came to rest on *Doktor* Ritter, the mysterious civilian whom he now knew was a key figure in the German Bay organization. He could see that Ritter did not share the rest's enthusiasm for the operation. He too seemed to find the thought of Operation Death Watch unpleasant. Why, Christian did not know.

'So, comrades,' von Arco broke into the chatter, rapping his pointer against the big map of the North Atlantic on the wall. 'Each individual skipper will take one of these grid squares between AI94 off Greenland down to BB90 between Halifax and St John's. It is our guess that it will be somewhere between the two that Roosevelt and Churchill will meet. It is also our belief that the *Prince of Wales's* security will be stricter than that of the presidential yacht. The *Prince of Wales* is unlikely to break radio silence while she has Churchill aboard and so give her position away. So, as I have already said, we will concentrate on the *Potomac*. Once we have located her – and I doubt with reporters and the like aboard that she will maintain radio silence – we will follow and close in with all available craft... Now then, gentlemen, I shall read out the names of you skippers and the grid squares to which you will be allotted. *Leutnant zur See Kammhuber.*'

'Sir!'

'You will sail to grid square…'

Slowly Ritter eased himself from the wall and while von Arco began to detail to a proud, eager Kammhuber what his task was to be in that area of the Atlantic, he left the room with apparent casualness. But Ritter's clever brain raced as he made his way through the great, glowing cave, loud with the clang of hammers and the hiss of torches, to the exit. For the first time the full magnitude of Operation Death Watch, with all its repercussions, whether the mission was successful or not, struck him; *and they were frightening!*

Now all the skippers were chatting excitedly, occasionally going over to the big wall map to check something in their own newly allotted grid squares, while Christian stood silent in their midst, for von Arco had still not given him his assignment. Indeed, in that vain, arrogant manner of his, he seemed to have forgotten Christian altogether. Of course, he was taking his revenge for the way Christian had snubbed him that day at the party on the *Lech*, he knew that. But still, he did command the U-69 and all boats available would be needed to carry out this operation. Finally, as von Arco made no move to speak to him, Christian swallowed his pride and said very formally, *'Kapitän-leutnant* von Arco – and the U-69?'

Von Arco took his time. He continued

talking to an excited Kammhuber for a few moments before turning and saying with feigned casualness, 'You wished for something, *Leutnant* Jungblut?'

Christian felt himself flushing with anger. He clenched his fists and controlled his temper with difficulty. 'My assignment, sir, for the U-69.'

'*Your* assignment?' von Arco echoed, savouring this moment of triumph, 'for the U-69?' He smiled coldly, but his eyes did not light up. 'But my dear Lieutenant Jungblut, there is no real need for you to know that at the present time.'

'No need to know, sir?' Christian said stupidly, not understanding. 'But I must if I am to prepare my boat and my crew.'

Then von Arco let him have it. 'But my dear Jungblut,' he said, the pleasure this gave him all too obvious on his face, 'it is no longer *your* boat and *your* crew!'

'But I don't understand, sir,' Christian stuttered, while the others stared at him and von Arco, aware that some sort of strange controversy was going on in front of their eyes, but unable quite to make out what it was. 'Captain Baer is long dead ... who else could...?'

'I am taking over the command of the U-69 personally, Jungblut. You will revert to executive officer. Now there are one or two things I want to discuss with my *skippers*.' He emphasized the word, turning the knife in the wound. 'I shall call for you when I need you, Jungblut. You are dismissed!' And with that he turned his back on a red-faced Christian and started to point out something on the map.

Blindly Christian staggered out of the room as half a mile away in German Bay, *Doktor* Ritter swung himself behind the wheel of the battered old Ford truck, his mind made up...

CHAPTER 3

MacKenzie stared hard at the aerial photograph, while Lejoly and the RCAF squadron leader who had rushed it to his office waited expectantly.

Outside, the rush-hour traffic was returning home and there was the usual angry honking of carhorns, as irate, hot, tired commuters blasted away at someone they thought was delaying their rush to get into casual, cooler clothes and hit that first bourbon.

The photo was not particularly good. As the squadron leader had explained five minutes earlier: 'It is a hand camera job, taken by the gunner of the Hudson concerned. Not a professional job, in other words.' It showed a barren area of scree, which had been oddly disturbed, as if it might have been hit by a sudden storm. There were odd deep furrows too, like those which might have been made by a drunken ploughman. There was one other detail of interest. In the instant that the unknown RCAF gunner had snapped the site, the sun had peeped through the fog and had glinted on something metallic in the corner of the place.

MacKenzie grunted and wordlessly Lejoly handed him a magnifying glass. MacKenzie stared at his subordinate. 'How did you know I wanted that?' he said gruffly.

'I'm no Sherlock Holmes, sir, if that's what you mean,' Lejoly replied and grinned. 'I just happened to notice the last time I visited you, you borrowed your wife's eyeglasses to read something. Hence the magnifying glass.'

'Too clever by half, Lejoly,' MacKenzie grunted. 'Ay, I'm getting old, mon. Won't be long now, Lejoly, and you'll be sitting behind this desk.' He focused the glass and stared hard at the photo once more, thinking aloud as he did so. 'Ye no need a crystal ball to figure that somebody has been working out there... Working to cover yon tracks... But what in tarnation are they? ... and what's that bit o' metal in the far corner?' He fiddled with the magnifying glass, trying to obtain the maximum focus for eyes which were growing old and tired. Suddenly he sucked in his breath sharply and said, 'There's a kind of wee white spot on the metal ... circular-shaped.'

The RCAF squadron leader tugged at his big moustache. 'My chaps had a quick look at it, sir, before I shot it over here, but they didn't notice anything. May I look, sir?'

'Ay, be my guest.' MacKenzie handed the photo and magnifying glass over to the young officer, who looked like a caricature of a British fighter pilot with his moustache and top button of his tunic undone.

Outside, a cop was shouting in a tough, angry voice, 'Willya get that frigging Chevy started, mister, or am I gonna have to frigging well have ya towed away?'

The squadron leader whistled softly and MacKenzie forgot the irate traffic cop. 'What is it?' he demanded quickly.

'Well, sir, if I'm not mistaken that's an RAF roundel on the piece of metal.'

'A roundel?' MacKenzie enquired.

'Yes, you know, sir, the RAF colours... Of course, you can't make the colours out, but I'll swear that's what it is, the RAF insignia in miniature.'

'You mean,' Lejoly said hastily, 'that that metal is aluminium, part of a plane, an RAF plane?'

'No.'

'Well, what kind of planc is it, if it is one in the first place?' MacKenzie snorted, feeling his blood pressure rising. Automatically he poured himself a shot of scotch, not caring whether the RCAF man saw him or not.

'Well, you know, sir, every time one of our boys has a kill, he has the fitters paint him up a black swastika on the tail of his kite, just to show what a wizard pilot he is.'

'Ay, ay, I've seen that in the movies,' MacKenzie agreed hastily. 'I ken what you mean.'

182

'And the Jerries do the same, sir. When they knock one of our kites out of the sky, they stick a little RAF sticker on their tail-planes and–'

'So, you mean,' Lejoly interrupted him urgently, 'that that's a German kite – er, plane down there?'

'I do indeed.'

MacKenzie tossed down his scotch in one throw and sprang to his feet. 'That explains the furrows and the mess of bushes and so on there. A plane crashed and they tried to cover it up the best they could. Underneath that foliage there's an airplane hidden – a *German* airplane!' He pushed his chair back, mind racing, and stalked across the hot stuffy office to the map of Quebec Province, Labrador and Newfoundland. 'Where exactly is yon site?' he barked.

The squadron leader passed hurriedly to the map and pointed. 'Up above the St Lawrence, sir. On the northern coast. Not too far from spam and dried egg field–'

'Where?' MacKenzie yelled.

The squadron leader smiled. 'Just the name our chaps gave to the landing field we had just up here, about twenty miles from German Bay.'

MacKenzie was intrigued enough to forget the urgency of his investigation for a moment and ask: 'But why spam and dried egg field?'

'Because when we were flying Yank aircraft

to the UK from there clandestinely, that's what their cargo mainly was – spam and dried eggs, and naturally nylons for the limey girls.'

'Naturally,' MacKenzie echoed. 'So we have a German aircraft crashing up there; not a hundred miles away further south we have an encounter with a mysterious German sub, which is probably seriously damaged, and thirdly we have the U-boats of the North Atlantic vanished from the ocean. Put it together and what do we have?'

The Squadron leader looked puzzled. Lejoly, however, clicked his fingers excitedly and snapped back, 'They're up there somewhere and they're up there because they're after Churchill!'

MacKenzie nodded grimly and for a moment a thick, leaden silence hung over the Inspector's office, broken only by the heavy ticking of the old-fashioned wall clock, ticking away the minutes of their life with metallic inexorability. Suddenly MacKenzie sprang into action with the impatient energy of a man half his age. 'Lejoly, note!' he snapped, craggy face almost wolfish and demanding.

Lejoly whipped out his notebook and pencil and said, 'Shoot, Inspector.'

'Signal chief of security, *Potomac*. Urgent President Roosevelt transfer to one of his escorts. Suggest the heavy cruiser *US*

Augusta. This will cut out any further press leaks from the *Potomac.*'

Lejoly scribbled furiously, while the squadron leader stood there, looking uncomfortable and out of place.

'Next, signal to HQ Canadian First Corps, Quebec. Request two battalions of motorized infantry immediately. Top priority from MacKenzie King himself. Immediate availability for operations along the Gulf of St Lawrence and Placentia Bay.'

Lejoly looked up. 'But you haven't got the Prime Minister's permission, sir,' he objected.

'Och, dinna fash yersen!' MacKenzie snarled in his broadest Scots accent. 'I'll nae doubt get it – *afterwards!* Now to the flag officer commanding St John's – you can find out his name afterwards, Lejoly: alert nearest destroyer flotilla. Enemy submarines suspected in Placentia Bay. Act on own initiative. Highest priority, as before, from MacKenzie King.' He grinned at a sweating and furiously scribbling Lejoly. The signals finished, he turned to the bemused squadron leader. 'Now then squadron leader, what can you brylcreem boys offer me?'

The RCAF officer looked slightly pained at the glib reference to the Air Force, but he answered promptly enough. 'There is a squadron of Hudson bombers on alert, sir, and at St John's we've got a flight of Swordfish torpedo bombers, which–'

'Sir!' an urgent voice from the door cut into his words.

MacKenzie swung round urgently. 'Did I nae say I wasna to be interrupted, Mac-Donald, eh?' he said angrily.

'I ken that, sir,' MacDonald answered, his broad Lowland Scots face flushed with embarrassment. 'But, sir, I told masen that this is vurry important … important enough to disturb the Inspector.'

'All right then, mon, spit it out. What is it?'

'Sir, we've just had a report, an urgent report, from one of our patrols… They say they have had a man surrender to them, voluntarily, who says he's a German agent.'

'*A what?*' MacKenzie exploded. Opposite him Lejoly stopped writing, his instincts telling him that this was the breakthrough they had been waiting for all along.

'Yessir,' MacDonald spluttered, 'and he knows all about the plan' – the big Scots sergeant's eyes seemed about to pop out of his head at any moment, as he fought to control his excitement – '*to murder Mr Churchill…!*'

CHAPTER 4

Glumly Christian stood on the clifftop over-
looking the bay shimmering in the brilliant
moonlight, listening to the muted klaxons
from below and the first throb of diesels.
Next to him Frenssen, equally as glum,
puffed at his cigarette and stared down at
the water, waiting for the first of the attack
force to appear.

Half an hour before, von Arco had made
his speech of departure, full of patriotic
rhetoric and resounding appeals for maximum efforts for 'Folk, Fatherland and
Führer'. Even the Russian artificers, their
work done at last, had apparently been
impressed. Then there had been the last
toast – in Canadian bourbon instead of the
usual schnapps – followed by three cheers
which had echoed and re-echoed through
the great cave before the crews had clattered
away to their boats. Now the two old comrades waited for the first boat to appear,
taking advantage of the night to escape
undetected into the open sea.

Christian dug his hands into the pockets of
his stiff grey leather suit and told himself
that although he disapproved of Operation

Death Watch, all the same he felt left out of things. Frenssen obviously thought the same, because he broke the heavy silence and said: 'Off they go to pit their strength against the frigging foe and all that sort of shit ... and we're gonna be left behind in his arsehole of the world, without any gash to pass the time with.' He dropped his cigarette onto the cropped turf and crushed it out angrily with his heavy cork-lined sea-boot.

Christian didn't say anything. Already the throb of the diesels was getting louder and there was a stink of oil now on the night breeze. Kammhuber would be first out, Christian told himself, the lucky bastard!

'Of course, you know what von Arco's game is, don't yer sir?' Frenssen said. Christian's mood was so depressed that he didn't have the heart to tell the big petty-officer to show more respect for his superiors. 'The U-69 could sail this very moment with the rest, in spite of that guff of his that she needs some more work. She's fuelled, provisioned, armed, all ready for a patrol. But Von Arco wants her to stay behind for his own reasons.'

Christian took his gaze off the bright silver water below. 'What reasons?'

'We know him of old, sir, don't we?' Frenssen said eagerly. 'He's got a yeller streak a metre wide. Remember what happened when he was our executive on the last patrol he ever did with us? He had his skivvies creamed all the time. So he's not going to risk his precious neck on this op. So what happens if it goes wrong, eh? What happens then?' He grunted angrily. 'I'll tell yer, sir. Von Arco's gonna use the U-69 for a quick bunk back to the Homeland, that's his game, mark my frigging words.' He spat contemptuously onto the ground.

Christian said nothing. He had already half-suspected the same thing. If the op succeeded von Arco would claim the credit for it. If anything went wrong, he had his personal escape route left open, thanks to the U-69.

From below there came a harsh bubbling sound and the stark, strangled whine of diesels being revved. Hastily Christian spun round and stared at the entrance to the cave. Short choppy waves were exploding down there. Kammhuber was coming out. A long, sleek sinister shape slid into view.

Christian and Frenssen clicked to attention, raising their gloved hands to their caps in salute as the crewmen doubled back and forth hurrying about their duties, while in the conning tower Kammhuber himself stood proudly surveying their work. Like a blond Nordic god he stood there, moisture dripping from his leather suit, eyes fixed on the dark sea horizon, as if he knew that some great destiny awaited him beyond it.

Christian dropped his hand, feeling almost sick with envy, as Kammhuber's boat began to gather speed and the next submarine made its appearance at the mouth of the cave, its bell signals ringing, small choppy waves dancing about its dark bow.

'Piss in the wind!' Frenssen said and dropped his hand too, as if he couldn't stand watching any more. 'Do you think we could get some suds or even a bit of sauce in that one-horse town over there?' He indicated the cluster of clapboard houses which made up German Bay, still lit here and there by yellow petroleum lamps; for there was no blackout on this side of the Atlantic. 'I could do with tipping something down my collar before turning in, sir.'

'Why not,' Christian said with faked heartiness. 'I could do with a stiff belt myself, even if it is in the company of a big rogue like yourself. Come on. Let's hoof it.'

Together they began to walk over the rough uneven grass, while below, boat after boat of that deadly wolf pack slid into the open sea and towards their meeting with destiny.

'You are named Klaus Ritter?' Inspector MacKenzie said in that dull routine manner he had acquired after twenty years in the Royal Mounted Police, although inside he raged, eager to check the man's initial evidence out.

'No,' the little man replied, his face too revealing nothing of his inner emotion, as they stared down at him in the yellow light in that remote provincial police station. 'Ritter is a *nom de guerre*. In my time I have had many names. But my real name is Dietz, Klaus.'

Lejoly made a quick note, and MacKenzie said, 'You are an American?'

Again the little man shook his head. 'No, but I wish to God I were! Then I would not be here this night. How fortunate the Americans–' He broke off and the impassioned look on his face vanished as quickly as it had appeared. 'I am a German citizen,' he said quietly.

'Now then Mr – er – Dietz, you stated to the sergeant that you are a German agent. Is this true?'

'Yes, I am a spy and have been these twenty years, ever since I left the German Navy at the end of World War One.'

Even MacKenzie was impressed. A spy who had survived two decades really was something. He made up his mind that the little man was not a crank and took the plunge, throwing the usual routine to the winds. 'If you are what you say you are, Mr Dietz, why have you turned yourself over to us? You must realize that we will regard you as an enemy alien and that you face a probable prison sentence for having carried out espionage activities on Canadian soil. I am making myself quite clear, am I not?'

The little man nodded and took another sip from the big cup of cold coffee and rum which he had been given half an hour before. 'I understand that perfectly, but I prefer a Canadian prison, for however long,' suddenly the little man smiled, showing a mouthful of sawn-off teeth, 'rather than a Canadian firing squad – or perhaps even a lynching.'

'A lynching?'

'Exactly, Inspector. If the German Navy succeeds in this operation, the western world will go wild. Those who are caught or surrender to the Canadians – and the Americans too – are not going to escape with a prison sentence. No sir,' the little man's face glowed with animation, showing the stress he was under, 'they'll be beating them to death in the streets!'

'Then it is true? They are going to attempt to kill Mr Churchill!'

The other man nodded and said simply, 'Yes.'

MacKenzie breathed out hard. At last he had been proved right. Lejoly smiled and, lowering his notebook, said, 'All right, Mr Dietz. I'll ask you one last question. Why, if you feared for your safety, didn't you simply cross the border into the States? That way you wouldn't have run the risk of facing a prison sentence as you now do here in Canada.' He paused and stared hard at the German, still trying to banish the lingering doubts he harboured. Was Dietz's confession the final phase of the German operation to throw them off the scent?

The little man took his time and his inner conflict was clearly revealed in his face. At the side of his left temple a nerve had begun to twitch and his lips moved as if he were carrying on some inner dialogue with himself. Finally he spoke: 'I am a loyal German, Inspector Lejoly,' he said slowly, measuring his words carefully as if what he had to say now was of great importance to him. 'Ever since I was a young officer in the Imperial Navy I have felt it was my most important duty to serve my Fatherland, in whatever way I could. But in recent years I have become increasingly disenchanted with the political rulers of my poor country. The Third Reich of Adolf Hitler is not the Germany I once knew and loved.' He stared hard at Lejoly and the latter could see the gleam of tears in the flickering yellow light of the petroleum lamp. He knew that the prisoner was telling the truth. Dietz's hurt was all too obvious. 'First the Jews, then the Czechs, the Poles, the Austrians ... oh, you know as well as I what I mean. This plot to kill Churchill was the last straw. It seemed to me to symbolize the mindless, perverted cruelty of the regime over there. When I heard them planning the attack on him, something snapped inside me–' He broke off abruptly and rubbed his eyes. 'I couldn't go along with it any longer, Inspector. That's why I came to you.' He hung his head, a defeated man.

MacKenzie pursed his lips and slowly unscrewed his hip flask. He deserved a drink, he told himself, and he didn't give a tinker's damn what the young Mountie sergeant thought of a superior who drank while he was on duty. 'Tomorrow, Saturday 9th August, 1941,' he said slowly, in between sips of the scotch, 'they meet: Roosevelt and Churchill. They tell me, Lejoly, it will be an historic occasion. I dinna ken much o' that. All I ken is that now they'll meet in safety and no harm'll come to yon grand old man.' He shook his head fondly, remembering those old days in Flanders with the flares flickering luridly over that nightmare landscape and the boys waiting on the parapet, bayonets fixed, eyes wild with excitement, and the guns thundering and the Colonel in that French tin hat he affected, drawing his pistol and crying in the heat of his blood, *'All right, boys, over the top – and be at 'em!'*

'Mr Dietz,' he said slowly, while the others stared at him, wondering what emotions were hidden by that old craggy face, 'when this business is finally over, I am recommending that you should be deported to the United States – a free man.' The little man stared at the Inspector in sheer disbelief. 'I also recommend to you that you set about becoming an American citizen as soon as you can, for to my way of thinking there will be no hope for Germany once the United States enters the war, which it undoubtedly will after tomorrow's meeting.' Suddenly he raised the flask, as if in a toast. *'God bless ye, Winston Churchill!'* he cried fervently and drained the rest of his scotch. Then he sat back, all energy drained from him as if a tap had been opened, his job done...

CHAPTER 5

'Verfluchtete Scheisse!' Kammhuber shrieked as the U-boat shook violently under the impact of a new burst of exploding depth-charges and started to rise, completely out of control. 'Stand by, deck crew!' he yelled, trying to keep control of himself as the cold water of the bay seeped in everywhere through buckled plates. The Tommies had caught them with their knickers down, almost as if they had known they were coming. They hadn't had a chance in the shallow water of the Bay of Placentia. A frantic Kammhuber turned his battered white cap back to front and ordered, *'Up periscope!'*

Swiftly he flung himself behind it as the crippled U-boat was struck by another pattern. The lights went out and someone screamed with fear. The boat started to flood with escaping gas. Even as the acrid fumes assailed his nostrils, Kammhuber knew that their electric batteries had been damaged. Now they could remain submerged no more. It was either fight it out on the surface or surrender. He slammed down the periscope handles and peered through the glass as the waves receded and the Bay became visible.

An amazing scene met his eyes. There were destroyers everywhere, dashing back and forth in frantic activity. To port there was a U-boat wallowing deep in the water, a white flag of surrender flying from her mast, her crew lining the deck with their hands raised. To starboard, lying there like a stranded metal whale, another U-boat was beached, smoke pouring from her, the dead scattered along her deck like broken, cast-aside dolls. 'God in heaven!' he gasped and fell back from the periscope as with a great gasp of escaping air the U-boat surfaced. 'They're slaughtering us out there. Radioman, signal to von Arco… Quick man! They caught the whole pack at the exit…' The rest of his words were drowned by the thunder of the first shell exploding against the conning tower with a great ear-splitting boom.

Kammhuber forgot von Arco. He clambered up the twisted ladder, followed by the rest of the deck crew. Desperately he heaved with all his strength to force the hatch. The deck crew tumbled madly into the open and pelted along the dripping deck to their gun. Kammhuber flung himself behind the twin machine-gun, crying into the voice-pipe as he spotted the destroyer heading straight for them, *They're going to ram us!*

The forward gun burst into life with a roar. Kammhuber dug the machine-gun hard into his shoulder. He pressed the trigger. At one thousand rounds per minute, it spat fire towards the enemy destroyer. The first German shell flung up a huge gout of whirling white water in front of the ship. It reeled violently, but still came on.

An enemy shell slammed into the submarine's bow. The gunners reeled back on all sides. Even as they fell, their riddled bodies were jetting scarlet blood. Red-hot slivers of metal hissed through the air. Kammhuber yelped with pain and clapped his hand to his shoulder. Suddenly his fingers were hot and sticky with blood. He fought the temptation to give in. 'Up second deck crew!' he heard himself order, as if he were listening to someone else. The men sped past him and, crouching low beneath the waves of tracer now scything the crippled submarine, pelted for the gun. Now the destroyer seemed to fill the world. Desperately, with fingers that felt like clumsy sausages, Kammhuber tried to load another belt of ammunition. He couldn't. He blinked his eyes several times. Nothing focused. The gun waved back and forth in the thick red mist that threatened to submerge him at any moment.

And then the monstrous great shape reared up above him. With the last of his strength he pressed the trigger. Harmlessly the bullets howled off the side of the destroyer in the same instant that her bow cleaved into the side of the submarine, shearing deep into her bow with a great rending and tearing of metal. Kammhuber reeled back, his ruined face dripping down onto his chest like a mess of molten red wax. The last of the attack force began to sink rapidly. The wolf pack had been destroyed...

'*Aircraft!*' von Arco cried fearfully, as the lines snaked through the air and crewmen ran up and down, watched by open-mouthed Russian technicians who worked no longer now that their guards had fled.

A sweating Christian cocked his head to one side. 'Sounds as if they were heading over us,' he rapped. 'Probably they're heading for the village. They'll take out German Bay first.'

'You mean,' von Arco quavered, his fear all too obvious, 'they *know* about us, Jungblut?'

Christian shrugged contemptuously. 'We'll soon know, won't we. If Ritter is a traitor, as you think, he might have learned that one boat remained behind. Now excuse me, I've got things to attend to if we're ever going to get out of this in one piece.'

He doubled away leaving von Arco to wring his hands like a frightened old woman as the first bombs started to drop on German Bay and the Russians scattered with fear.

'Listen to me,' Christian snapped, looking around those in the conning tower: Hinrichs, Frahm, the engineer, and Frenssen, 'Von Arco is nominally Skipper of the U-69, but only nominally.' He poked his thumb angrily at his own chest. 'I'm in charge until we get back to the Homeland. *Klar?*'

'*Klar!*' they snapped back as one and Christian could see from the looks in their eyes that he had their full support.

'We're not surrendering and we're not going to be sunk,' he continued firmly, as the detonation of the bombs whipped up the oily water at the exit to the cave and the cranes trembled under their impact. 'We're going to make it. Now, as soon as we exit we're going to dive. It's our only chance. It's going to be a matter of split-second timing. Dive and immediate silent running. It's going to be hell trying to get out of the bay, but we'll do it, if everyone keeps his ner–'

The sudden burst of machine-gun fire cut into his words with startling suddenness. A line of slugs leapt across the concrete ramp kicking up a series of angry blue sparks. One of the Russians flung up his arms dramatically as they ripped his chest apart, hands clutching the air as if he were climbing the rungs of an invisible ladder.

'Shit on the shingle,' Frenssen cried. '*Tommies...* Look!' Heavily armed men in khaki were clambering down the ladders that ran into the cave, some of them firing as they came.

Christian didn't hesitate. 'Come on, they're on to us!' he yelled. *'Frenssen, hold them off for Chrissake!'*

'Frigging buck-teeth Tommies!' the big petty officer yelled with sudden anger and, swinging the conning tower machine-gun around as if it was a toy, he ripped off a tremendous burst.

The Canadian soldiers came skidding to a sudden stop, men dropping everywhere in a mass of flailing arms and legs. Christian didn't wait to see any more. 'Von Arco,' he yelled above the noise, the screams of the wounded and the panic-stricken yells of the fleeing Russians, *'los* ... we're off, man... *Los!'*

Von Arco looked wildly from the Canadians to the big *Obermaat* swinging the machine-gun back and forth, cursing wildly as if he couldn't comprehend what was going on. Christian didn't hesitate. He ran across, grabbed the other officer by the arm and propelled him forward as the Canadians opened fire again. 'Come on, frig you!' he hissed, beside himself with anxiety and rage.

A grenade sailed through the air. Hastily Christian ducked, dragging an ashen-faced von Arco with him. The bomb spun over their heads and slammed into the side of the conning tower. It exploded in a burst of angry red flame. Hinrichs screamed, high and hysterical, and went down, what looked

201

like a mess of strawberry jam streaming down his face. He was dead before he hit the deck.

Christian thrust past him, propelling von Arco in front of him. 'Get below, you yellow bastard,' he snarled and gave the other man an angry shove. Von Arco tumbled down the ladder. Hastily Christian yelled into the voice-pipe as the Canadians began to advance on the U-69, firing from the hip as they doubled in and out of the cranes, crates and the litter of this secret dockyard: *'Both engines half ahead!'*

Frantically the deck-hand at the bow flung off the last cable and the next moment went down to his knees, his chest stitched suddenly with bloody buttonholes.

Slowly, maddeningly slowly, the U-69 started to move from its berth, with Christian physically willing it to clear the cave before the Canadians overran it, his knuckles gripping the edge of the conning tower white with tension. Next to him, Frenssen fired to left and right, trying to keep the Canadians back.

All was noise and confusion now. Shouts, wailing sirens, the snap crackle of small-arms fire, punctuated by the *boom-boom* of the bombs dropping on German Bay. The entrance to the cave loomed ever larger. Beyond, the sky was grey with early morning fog. Christian breathed a sigh of relief.

At least they'd have a little cover out there. He tensed over the voice-pipe as the slugs howled off the conning tower, ready to give the order to dive once they had cleared the cave.

To their right, a gigantic Canadian loomed up out of the smoke. In his hands he carried a clumsy-looking weapon that Christian, his heart beating frantically, could only guess was some kind of anti-tank gun. 'Frenssen,' he yelled desperately, 'over here–'

The Canadian fired. What looked like a metal bomb came hurtling towards the U-69. Christian ducked instinctively as the missile whacked into the side of the U-boat and exploded with a tremendous roar. The U-69 shook violently. One of the deck crew gave a panic-stricken scream and disappeared over the side. Next moment the screws caught his body and chewed it to pulp, leaving a blood-red wake to follow the hard-pressed submarine.

'Great buckets of flying ordure!' Frenssen cursed as the Canadian fired again and the missile slammed into the U-69's bow, tearing a great jagged hole in it. *'Sod this for a frigging tale!'* He spun the conning tower machine-gun around and rattled off a tremendous burst. The Canadian's chest was ripped apart. Suddenly it was a mass of bright-red blood, flecked here and there with brilliant white bone that gleamed like

polished ivory. Frenssen did not stop. He snapped off another burst, deliberately aiming yet lower on the dying man's body, crying furiously as he was carried away by the crazed blood-lust of battle. 'See how your frigging outside plumbing likes this, *Tommy!*'

The Canadian flew backwards and slammed into a gantry, arms outspread like a latter-day Christ, his sexual organs a mass of bloody gore; and there he hung in his dying agony like some grim memento of their passing, as the U-69 burst out into the grey foggy dawn beyond...

CHAPTER 6

Churchill, wearing his siren suit, lit his first Havana cigar of the day standing on the Admiral's bridge, staring out over the water of the bay. It was a cold grey morning, but the wind had dropped and this Saturday morning the sea was calm. 'Can you see any sign of them?' he asked the duty officer eagerly.

'The American destroyers, sir?' the young flag officer asked.

'Yes.'

'Not yet, sir, but they should be arriving soon. And sir,' he could not contain the good news any longer, though he knew well he might get a rocket from the Skipper for telling Churchill without the captain's permission, 'there have been some tremendous developments overnight, sir.'

'Pray inform me then,' Churchill said grandly, wondering a little at the young officer's excitement after a long, dreary pre-dawn watch.

'The Royal Canadian Navy destroyed at least seven Jerry subs early this morning, sir! Sunk 'em not fifty miles away from here, sir. A tremendous show!' He grinned at the Prime Minister, full of youthful exuberance.

'Apparently, sir,' he continued, 'the Jerries had established a secret sub base at a remote spot on the Canadian mainland. Their authorities became aware of it, knocked it out and the subs that were operating from it.'

Churchill returned his smile. It was a good omen for his meeting with the Former Naval Person. It would be the first thing he would tell Roosevelt when he met him.

Now the *Prince of Wales* was steaming towards the wide inland sea, ahead the outline of a grey and lonely land, a low silhouette of hills touched with mist.

'The Yanks – er – Americans, sir!' the young flag officer cried suddenly, as Churchill gazed at the desolate scene. 'Can you see, sir? Over there!' He offered Churchill his telescope. Obediently Churchill took it and focused, as the young officer called out the names of the American warships. 'That one is the cruiser *Augusta,* sir, with the President aboard... That's the cruiser *Tuscaloosa* over there and the battleship with all those masts ... that's the *Arkansas.'*

'Arkan*saw*,' Churchill corrected his pronunciation, grateful suddenly that he had had an American mother who had taught him such things.

Now American seaplanes and destroyers began to steam out to the great weather-beaten British battleship with its striped camouflage.

Churchill focused his glass on the awning that had been erected on the forward gun turret of the *Augusta*. A tall man stood there in a light-brown suit, scrutinizing the *Prince of Wales* for his first glimpse of Churchill. The Prime Minister's heart leapt. That one man would soon help to decide the fate of the British Empire. Without America's help, Britain could not win this war; everything depended upon his ability to convince Roosevelt not only to keep sending supplies to a hard-pressed Britain, but also to take an active part in the fighting against Germany.

Now, as the battered *Prince of Wales* passed through the lines of gleaming, polished American ships, Churchill felt the gulf of experience. The American craft, with their shining brass and pine-white woodwork, were so obviously the ships of a nation at peace. How could they understand the grim years of battle that Britain had already spent since that September of 1939?

On the quarter deck, the bosuns' whistles shrilled and the band of the Royal Marines crashed into the *Star Spangled Banner*. Like an echo across the strip of water came the slower, more sedate notes of *God Save The King*. On the *Augusta*, the President raised his panama in salute. Churchill did the same.

So the warship passed to her anchorage, where a flag on a buoy rose above the water.

For a moment, as the bands thundered and the whistles shrilled, it seemed that the *Prince of Wales* might cut it down. Then, at the instant of touching it, the warship slowed and with a tremendous rattle of rusty metal the anchor chains descended into the water. The Prime Minister had arrived in Placentia Bay. It was nine o'clock on the morning of Saturday 9th August, 1941...

Tense with excitement, heart beating like a trip-hammer, Christian stood in the conning tower as they emerged into the grey dawn. Up on the heights, German Bay blazed. The drone and whine of aircraft engines drowned even the throbbing of their diesels and the snap and crackle of small-arms fire from within the cave as the Canadian Spitfires came hurtling out of the blazing sky to machine-gun the panic-stricken survivors fleeing their burning village.

Fingers gripping the edge of the conning tower in white-knuckled tension, Christian waited till they had sufficient depth to dive, knowing that the enemy planes would discover them at any moment. Up on the bow, the lookout sang out the depths, while behind him Frenssen, furiously feeding another long, gleaming belt of ammunition into the machine-gun, waited for the aerial attack which *had* to come.

The first Canadians came running out of

the exit to the cave along the line of slippery wet rocks, firing from the hip. Leading Hand Trees took aim, arm behind his back, pistol outstretched as if he was one some peacetime firing range. He pulled his trigger. The pistol jerked upwards and the leading Canadian threw up his arms, pirouetted in a grotesque travesty of a ballet-dancer and slammed into the wet rocks.

Trees swung round, youthful face full of eager pride. 'How's that, sir, for the close combat badge?' he cried in the same instant that the Spitfire zoomed over the edge of the cliff, eight machine-guns spitting death. Trees gave a shrill scream, clutching his chest frantically as the slugs ripped the length of it. He was dead before he hit the bottom of the conning tower.

Frenssen gave a great bellow of rage. He swung the gun round and fired a furious burst at the Spitfire. Tracer cut through the air in lethal fury. To no avail! The enemy fighter plane zoomed effortlessly into the grey sky, trailing thick black smoke behind it.

Furiously Christian flung a glance below. Von Arco's craven face stared up at him, eyes wild with unreasoning fear. 'Get out of my frigging way!' Christian shrieked, beside himself with rage at the death of Trees, the trap the U-69 found itself in, the whole rotten, bloody business of war!

Von Arco flew back. The engineer officer flashed a look upwards. He knew what Christian wanted without being asked. 'It's going to be nip-and-tuck!' he cried, 'to dive in these shallows. There–'

The rest of his words were drowned by the roar of another enemy fighter diving in at four hundred miles an hour, machine-guns chattering frenetically. A lookout screamed and disappeared over the side, swept away by the tremendous leaden hail.

'We can't wait any longer!' Christian yelled. 'All right, you deck people ... we're going to dive. Hurry now. *Dalli ... dalli!*' They needed no urging. Already a third plane was circling high above them, ready to make its attack, and the two that had already attacked the U-69 were zooming round in a tight curve, ready to follow suit.

Madly the deck men clattered towards the conning tower. Behind Christian, Frenssen swung round his gun to meet the new attack. 'Get below, *Obermaat!*' Christian yelled above the snarl and howl of aircraft engines.

Frenssen, squinting down the long, air-cooled barrel, ignored the order. 'I'm going to take one of the frigging bacon-and-eggs bastards with me before I go!' he snarled wolfishly. 'Come on, pig-fucker ... come to daddy!'

Christian leant to one side as the excited deck crew began to clatter down the ladder.

The howl of engines grew ever louder. He flashed a glance over the side. He could no longer see the bottom of the sound. Was the water deep enough? *God in heaven, make it deep enough for the boat to dive!*

Frenssen's machine-gun erupted into crazy life. The spitfire in the lead of the attack seemed to stop in mid-air, as if it had run into an invisible wall. For a moment it hung there foolishly, nothing seemingly happening. Suddenly it disintegrated. Fragments of a wing spiralled down like metal leaves. With a howl of protesting metal, the Spitfire hurtled to the ground and smashed into the hillside.

'*Hurrah!*' Frenssen began.

'*Hurrah my arse!*' Christian yelled above the racket. He grabbed him by the shoulder and virtually flung him down the hatchway. Next moment he was clattering after him, sliding the last metre down the sides of the ladder, to secure the hatch with fingers that trembled violently. '*Dive … dive … dive!*' he cried fervently, as someone slung Hinrich's dead body into the corner as if it were a bundle of sodden old rags.

'*Twenty … thirty metres … forty … forty-five metres!*' the engineer officer sang out, as the U-69 began to dive, the electric motors whining as they took over. Now Christian shook his head to dislodge the sweat drops that threatened to blind him, gaze fixed hypnotically on the depth gauge, knowing that even now the Spitfires, cheated of their prey, would be radioing bombers and surface craft to take over before the U-69 could escape into the wider area of the bay. How he might escape through the only two exits to Placentia Bay with the whole of the enemy air force and navy alerted, God only knew. He forced that thought out of his mind and concentrated on the task in hand. 'First things first,' he whispered to himself and ordered, 'Sixty metres – easy!'

The boat levelled out straight away, the trim perfect. Now they surged ahead at a steady eight knots, everything seemingly routine and straightforward. But the faces of the crew reflected their inner tension as they poised there in the strange green-glowing gloom, the sweat beading their foreheads like drops of dew.

Suddenly the boat bucked like a wild horse being put to the saddle for the first time. Glass shattered. Here and there a plate buckled and seawater surged in. Someone cursed and picked himself up from a suddenly littered floor. Von Arco cringed, putting his fingers to his mouth like a terrified, hysterical woman.

'Aerial bomb,' Christian announced, trying to make his voice sound calm and routine. 'Not a depth-charge.' He flung a look at the depth gauge, knowing that even in the grey gloom of the early morning he might well still be visible to a bomber hovering over the bay. 'Take her down to ninety … easy now.'

Delicately, almost as if he were playing some incredibly ancient and highly-priced instrument, Frahm, the engineer, adjusted the controls, knowing that the water was so shallow that he might well rip the keel of the U-69 to pieces on the bottom of the bay if he miscalculated. Slowly but steadily the submarine began to sink another thirty metres, the blue needle edging its way round ever so carefully. There was another thud, but much more muted now. The U-69 shuddered as the bomb exploded, but no longer so fearsomely as before.

'Ninety it is, sir,' Frahm called, voice subdued as if their hunters on the surface might well be able to overhear them.

'Thank you, Chiefie,' Christian answered, radiating a confidence that he did not altogether feel. 'I think we've done it this time.'

Now the U-69 moved forward silently, getting ever deeper into the bay as their relentless hunters sped towards them...

CHAPTER 7

It was fifteen minutes later that the Canadian destroyers found them.

There was the first muffled thud of a depth-charge and then it was as if a gigantic fist had just slammed into the U-69. Standing in the control room Christian felt a sudden upsurge in his knee-joints and he had to grab a stanchion to prevent himself from falling. The needle of the depth gauge jumped alarmingly. Someone yelled. There was the tinkle of glass and in an instant the lights went out.

'Put on yer party frocks, ladies,' Frenssen yelled, trying to calm the greenbeaks, 'the dance has just frigging well started!'

The emergency lights flickered on the next moment and 'the dance' commenced.

Christian's mind raced electrically. Opposite him von Arco, squatting on the tarpaulin-wrapped bundle which was poor Ensign Hinrich's dead body, stared at him in open-eyed terror. Surrender was written all over his craven face. Christian bared his teeth in contempt. There was going to be no surrender. But where to hide? What to do? *Ascend? Descend? Switch to port? Switch to starboard? Stop running altogether and sweat it out until they went away?*

As another pattern of depth-charges rocked the boat from side to side as if it were a child's toy and the first stink of acrid smoke began to seep into the control room, Christian ordered full ahead, same course. That might put the Tommies off. They'd expect anything but that.

'Fire below!' Frahm reported, voice low and apparently quite calm.

'Probably leads smouldering. *Obermaat,* check it out – at the doub–'

Christian grabbed desperately for a stanchion as the boat was buffeted again by another salvo of the damned depth-charges. His first manoeuvre had failed. 'Take her down!' he rasped. Opposite him, lips quavering like some village idiot, von Arco was weeping, great tears of self-pity rolling down his ashen face.

'She's not stable, sir!' Frahm objected hurriedly.

'Risk we've got to take! *Take her down!*'

'Yessir.'

Four thuds in quick succession. Four great hammer blows struck the hull of the hard-pressed boat. Frenssen did not seem to notice as he fought the fire, a blood-red giant in the reflected glow of the flames that leapt up about his knees.

'One hundred and twenty fathoms!'

215

Frahm sang out.

'Good,' Christian yelled above Frenssen's obscene cursing, 'another forty and then to port!'

The minutes passed in leaden tension. Frenssen, lathered in sweat, the legs of his pants singed, was controlling the fire now. As the U-69 swung to port at a completely different depth, the pale-faced crew waited for the next pattern to hit them. Had they thrown the enemy off? Even Frenssen stopped cursing. Holding on to the stanchion, Christian tensed his stomach muscles, chill beads of perspiration running down the small of his back, his damp underpants sticking to his crotch unpleasantly. Suddenly there they were. *One ... two ... three ... four...!* The insane gurgle of boiling, churning water. The roar as the bombs exploded. But they were behind them and this time the U-boat rocked quite gently. Frahm swallowed hard and looked across at Christian who dared now to take his hand away from the supporting stanchion. 'I think ... I think, sir,' he said in a strained, hoarse voice, 'that we might have ... thrown them off, sir.'

Christian nodded his agreement. He could not do otherwise. Somehow his voice would not function.

Now they moved full ahead, floating silently in the depths of the bay. Up on the surface, the frustrated Canadians sought

216

them desperately. There was the sound of what appeared to be a handful of gravel flung along the length of the hull.

'Asdic,' Frenssen whispered, wiping the sweat off his blackened face. 'The frigging apeturds are still after us!'

'Yes,' Christian replied, already attempting to plan his next move to put their hunters off the scent, 'the Tommies don't give up that easily. Now keep quiet. Silent running everybody!'

Now the pressure became almost intolerable. When would the Tommies find them? All conversation had died away. There was no sound save the soft hum of the electric motors and the persistent irritating *drip-drip* of a leak somewhere. Mutely, like dumb animals they waited for the slaughter.

Another shower of gravel. The hydrophone operator whispered his report, 'Propeller noises, sir ... bearing two-zero-zero, sir... Getting louder...' They waited again. 'Getting louder...' the tense, sweating operator repeated his findings.

A tremendous explosion close by. 'Here we go agen!' Frenssen yelled in alarm, as the U-69 rocked and lurched convulsively, the enraged water tossing it back and forth as if it were a weightless feather.

Opposite a white-faced Christian, von Arco clutched his throat as if he were choking, face suddenly scarlet, head twisted to one side like that of a man being slowly strangled. 'I can't stand it any more!' he gasped, the saliva running down the side of his mouth. 'We've got to give up... Surface, there is no other way we can–'

Christian reached out and dealt him a savage blow across the face so that he reeled back against the bulkhead. 'Shut up!' he hissed. 'Do you want to panic the poor sods? They're suffering enough as it is!' Von Arco hung his head and began to whimper like a favourite dog beaten by his adored master.

Christian made his decision. It was no use attempting simply to lie there submerged. They couldn't bluff the Tommies like that. It was obvious they were persistent swine and knew that the U-boat was virtually trapped in the bay. Fortunately for the U-69 the destroyers had to fire their depth-charges at speed. If they had been able to creep up slowly, locate the U-69 immediately by asdic and drop their charges in that very same instant, this lethal cat-and-mouse game would have been over at once. But they couldn't. Christian knitted his brow in concentrated thought as he forced his mind to go through a series of chess moves which could have a deadly and very final outcome if he made a wrong one.

Another salvo. The U-69 swayed crazily from side to side. They had been located again. 'Hard-a-port... Full ahead, *both!*' Christian snapped, instinctively giving the right order. *'Schnell!'*

The boat lurched forward, the din echoing and re-echoing, with ratings grabbing hold of pipes and stanchions for dear life as she surged on at high speed.

Christian knew that the enemy captains could not keep the U-69 pin-pointed at high speed. But they *would* know that the submarine would jink to either port or starboard, or vary the depth. These were the three possibilities they would assume. There was also another that Christian was still toying with at the back of his mind, although the problems of the moment were paramount: through which channel would the U-boat attempt to exit from Placentia Bay, *if* it succeeded in evading its present pursuers? My God, he cursed to himself, one needed the brains of a damned Einstein to compute all the myriad possibilities! Then he had it. 'Take her up to thirty metres!' he ordered, surprised at his own boldness.

Someone gasped. Frahm stared at him and Frenssen said, 'But if they've got aircraft up there'

'They won't have, you big rogue,' Christian cut him short. 'And even if they have, they won't be flying low enough to see us. Why,' he chortled, suddenly very pleased with himself, 'if one of those damned depth-charges hit them while they were flying low, they'd get an awful case of piles!'

'Of course,' Frahm agreed, abruptly enthusiastic, 'if there are any aircraft up there, they'll certainly be keeping their distance from the destroyers.' He bent over his controls, suddenly full of new energy and hope. 'Thirty metres it is, sir,' he sang out. Slowly the U-69 started to rise...

Now the eager sailors of the *Prince of Wales* saw a line of motor boats approaching the stationary battleship, a pyramid of cigarette cartons piled in the stern of each of the spotless white American craft. Everywhere they crowded the decks of the great battleship, shouting and cat-calling in good-natured excitement, while the press photographers, British and American, mingled nervously with the hard-bitten tars ready to take the required propaganda pictures for the people back home.

The first launch was unloaded and the sailors stepped forward smartly to receive their parcels of cigarettes, cheese and fruit, each one bearing the legend: 'The President of the United States sends his compliments and best wishes'.

Churchill watched in high good humour, crying to a group of the American sailors who had brought the gifts, 'Come over here.' Taking charge, he grouped them with a number of British sailors and eyed the group critically before growling to the photographers: 'How's that?'

'Very good, sir,' they said in unison. They raised their heavy cameras.

Churchill stopped them with an imperious gesture. 'Wait a moment, don't take it yet,' he ordered. Waving his cigar at the sailors, he shouted: *'More teeth!'* The sailors burst out laughing and the photographers started clicking away happily, knowing that picture would make the front pages of the western world's newspapers on the morrow.

For a moment Churchill watched the young American sailors in their spotless whites, reflecting how well-fleshed and fed they looked in comparison with the men of the *Prince of Wales.* They belonged to peacetime still: to the prosperous, easy world full of advertisements for every conceivable food; gleaming new automobiles, new clothes, luxury, a world where money still meant almost everything.

His gaze left the happy sailors and the busy photographers. His eyes swept to the shore, where a lone yellow light still burned among the deserted bays and barren hills, that of some lone crofter perhaps, he told himself. But how could one describe the heart-catching beauty of that sight? All Europe was dark and had been for nearly three years now; yet here in this lonely land, women had never caught their infants to their breasts in fear and men had never crouched like animals in the dark, listening to the sound of the enemy above them in the sky, waiting in tense expectation for that first dreaded whine of the bombs.

'Sir,' a voice broke into his reverie.

He turned, a little startled. It was the flag officer of the early morning and he was just as excited as he had been then. 'Well, young man, what is it? I would have thought you would have been off watch.'

'I was, sir. But the Skipper ordered me back on duty. There has been a new development.'

'New development?' Churchill echoed. 'What new development?'

'We didn't get all the Jerry subs yesterday. One of them has so far managed to dodge the RCN and their air force.'

'Hm, and where is this Hun craft?'

'Still here in the Bay, sir... We think. Our guess is that she'll attempt to break through our cordon, if she's still not been destroyed by then, to the north between the northern tip of Newfoundland and Canada.'

'But why not here? If my memory serves me correctly, the exit to Placentia Bay here is some sixty miles in breadth.'

'You're quite correct, sir. Sixty-*two* to be exact. But sir,' the young flag officer spread out his arm expansively, sweeping in the great mass of American ships riding at anchor, with the busy motor launches and pinaces swarming back and forth between them, 'even the craziest U-boat skipper wouldn't dare to run the gauntlet of this lot, would he, sir?' he objected. 'He wouldn't have a cat's chance in hell!'

Churchill mused for a moment, stroking his pugnacious jaw in that well-remembered manner of his. 'I suppose you are right, young man,' he concluded after a while.

'But still, we are taking all precautions, sir,' the other man went on eagerly, adrenaline suddenly pumping at the thought of the new danger. 'Tonight, the American ships will black out, just as we do. Not only that, but the shore is going to be ordered to black out too, with effect from twenty-two hundred hours, sir.'

Suddenly Churchill looked impressed, so much so that the young flag officer stopped his flood of words, slightly bewildered. Had he said anything wrong; anything that had displeased the great man?

He hadn't. Indeed Churchill, impressionable and emotional as he always was, given to sudden tears and moods of black despair, was entranced by the young man's announcement. He raised his finger, as if in warning, and growled, 'Don't you see, Lieutenant? It is that symbolic gesture that I have been looking for all the time during this long cruise to the New World!'

The flag officer swallowed hard. 'Not really, sir,' he stuttered.

But the question was a rhetorical one. Now Churchill's blue eyes were fixed on a horizon that was known only to him. 'This night,' he pronounced, voice heavy, solemn and significant, 'a European darkness will descend on Placentia Bay and the North American mainland. It is a sign. Before this year of 1941 is out, it will not just be the blackout, it will be the whole thing... The United States Army will be at war, fighting at our side. We are saved – *at last!*'

Next to him, the young man who had exactly five more months to live shivered, he knew not why...

CHAPTER 8

'Have we done it, Skipper?' Frenssen whispered, breaking the tense silence of the last fifteen minutes, which had seemed to Christian more like fifteen years.

Christian took his time. They had had no asdic 'gravel' for that period and the hydrophone operators had reported no propeller sounds during that same time. 'There's only one way to find out, *Obermaat,*' he said, putting an optimism into his voice for the sake of the crew that he did not feel.

'Take her up, sir?'

Christian nodded. 'Take her up,' he echoed and then snapped, 'periscope height, please!' There was a gasp from the ratings and even von Arco stopped his broken whimpering.

Slowly, almost painfully, the U-69 rose towards the surface, Frahm using all his experience and cunning, his gaze fixed almost hypnotically on the trim so that no one part of the submarine broke the surface before the rest, his face glazed with sweat. 'Periscope height,' he said.

'Trim?'

'Perfect, sir.'

'Thank you, chiefie.'

Frahm blushed with pleasure and lowered his eyes for a moment, 'Like a vestal virgin when she's seeing a bit o'male salami for the first time!' as a relieved Frenssen commented a little later.

Christian wasted no more time. 'Up periscope!' he commanded, voice firm and determined. But he was cautious all the same. This time he squatted on his knees so that he would have to take it up only to the very minimum height to see just above the surface of the bay. A moment later the lens broke clear of the water, pivoting only millimetres above it. Slowly at low power he swept the grey swell, tensed for the first glimpse of smoke or a masthead which would indicate danger. Nothing! He switched to high power. Immediately normal vision was magnified four times. The objects around him seemed to leap towards him. Again nothing. He swivelled the handle and turned it so that he was looking at the sky right overhead. *Empty!* 'Down periscope,' he said in a matter-of-fact voice, while the crew waited anxiously for his verdict, their gazes fixed on him as if mesmerized. He took his time before saying slowly, 'Nothing. Comrades, we've lost them!'

'Did you hear that, you bunch of piss-pansies!' Frenssen broke the heavy silence with a great roar. 'We've lost 'em! *We've lost the English shiteheels!*'

'Three cheers for the Skipper!' Frahm cried. 'Hip, hip, *Hurrah!*'

'*HURRAH!*' the whole crew bellowed out the cheer, the relief all too obvious on their wan, worn faces. Even von Arco stopped his whimpering and began to look about him like someone who had just woken from a long, heavy sleep.

Christian beamed for a moment, happy with himself and with them, the men whose lives lay in his hands, telling himself that there wasn't a crew in the whole of the *Kriegsmarine* finer than this bunch of old hares and greenbeaks. For a few seconds he indulged himself in a kind of soft sentimentality foreign to his nature, a sort of warm comradeship with his hunted men deep below the sea in the midst of the enemy camp. Then he pulled himself together, knowing they were not out of trouble yet by a long chalk. 'Comrades, shipmates,' he said sternly, 'we have won phase one of the battle to get home, but there is still phase two to come.' He let his words sink in for a moment, watching the happy looks vanish from their faces to be replaced by expressions of earnest attention. 'There are two ways out of Placentia Bay. The narrow outlet to the north and the ninety-kilometre broad one to the south. Now our enemies know that we are still within the Bay and will have to escape through one of those two exits. If we are unfortunate, they will divide their forces between the two.' He paused. 'I think they *won't* because they'll need a devil of a lot of planes and ships to cover the southern outlet on account of its size. So, God willing, they will concentrate their forces. Now *where* will they concentrate them?'

'In the southern outlet,' Frahm ventured, 'because they will reason that with so much sea space we will take it? It will give us much more chance of escaping?'

'Ay, that will be it,' some of the crew agreed.

Christian pursed his lips hesitantly and said, 'I agree in a way. But in another I don't.'

'How do you mean, sir?' Frenssen asked.

'The southern escape route is so obvious, and whatever else you can say about the Tommies, this one thing is for sure, they are a cunning, devious race. Will they fall for the obvious?' There was a mutter of agreement among the old hares who had been fighting the British since 1939. 'So comrades, shipmates, I have decided this. We shall make for the northern exit. There we will prepare a trap for the Tommies, if they are waiting for us there.'

'A trap?' von Arco asked dully.

Christian ignored him. 'We'll fake a U-boat killing, making it so obvious that they'll know we're faking it. Some of your old duds, bilge oil, and,' he broke off and looked at

Hinrichs's body wrapped in the black tarpaulin, 'poor Ensign Hinrichs. They'll all go out through a torpedo tube this night just short of that northern outlet. Then we'll surface and go all out on our diesels, hoping to reach the southern outlet by dawn. We'll exit through it submerged.' Christian saw the sudden looks of doubt on their pale faces and said urgently, 'It is the only way, comrades.'

'Of course we'll make it, you lot of cardboard sailors,' Frenssen snorted contemptuously. 'Them buck-teethed Tommies'll have to get up a frigging lot earlier in the morning to catch our Skipper.'

Silently Christian prayed that *Obermaat* Frenssen was correct. Aloud, he said, 'Well, comrades, let's snap to it. We've got a long night in front of us...'

The PM had wept that morning as they had stood together in the still breeze, British and American, to sing the old hymns. Roosevelt had been unaffected. But even his craggy face had softened in the end. It had been the benediction that had done it: that slow, solemn benediction that was ordered to be said every day in the Royal Navy. It had begun with that well-remembered phrase, *'O Eternal Lord God, Who alone spreadest out the heavens, and rulest the sea...'* and ended with the plea, *'Preserve us from the dangers of the sea and from the violence of the enemy; that we may be a security for such as pass upon the seas upon their lawful occasions; that the peoples of the Empire may in peace and quietness serve Thee, our God; and that we may return in safety to enjoy the blessings of the land, with the fruits of our labours...'*

'I think I stage-managed it exceedingly well,' Churchill said expansively, waving his cigar at the admiring crowd which filled the wardroom, the tears of the morning forgotten now. 'The bands, the hymns, *the whole shoot,* as our cousins from across the sea would call it, were all calculated to remind the Former Naval Person of our common heritage.' He dipped the end of his big cigar in brandy and gave a tremendous puff on it, obviously well-pleased with himself. 'We shall confer all day Monday,' he continued, 'but that is a mere formality.' He pointed his cigar at the assembled brass almost as if he were levelling a deadly weapon at them. 'But what I wanted is already in the bag. I have a feeling that something is going to happen soon, something very big.' His eyes twinkled excitedly. 'Perhaps the first thing necessary, I told myself before I came here, before two great nations can fight together for the second time in one generation is to raise a standard. It was George Washington who said: "Let us raise a standard to which the wise and honest can repair. The rest is in the hands of God."' Churchill paused dramatic-

230

ally. 'Gentlemen, this day we have raised that standard between our two nations, the Anglo-American Standard! God willing, before this year of 1941 is over, we shall be bearing it together in common battle.' He sat back, as if suddenly exhausted, looking the very old man he was.

Captain Pym, toying with his pink gin right at the back of the crowd of brass-hats, frowned. The Premier might think he had raised a standard, but would he ever be able to return home to bear that standard? There was still a U-boat loose in Placentia Bay and Intelligence from London had signalled that *Radio Berlin* had reported Roosevelt and Churchill to have met off Newfoundland. It was pretty certain that once the *Prince of Wales* sailed on Wednesday she would encounter U-boats. Even if they *were* able to dodge the U-boats, there was still the grave danger of air attack once the battleship approached home waters and the German fields on the coast of occupied Europe.

But if Pym was worried about the future, Churchill was not. He roused himself from his sudden lethargy and said, as the attentive steward filled his glass hurriedly, 'Gentlemen, I would like to ask you to raise your glasses.' Hastily the company did so. 'To this great meeting at Placentia Bay which marks for ever in the pages of history the taking up of the common cause of the

English-speaking nations. Placentia Bay!'

'Placentia Bay!' the company echoed solemnly.

Churchill waited till the glasses were refilled before speaking again. 'And to you, gentlemen, of His Majesty's *Prince of Wales*, who have braved the perils of the sea to make it possible. To the crew of the *Prince of Wales!*'

They drank and as they did so, the old man watched their faces, as if trying to imprint them on his mind's eye for ever: the stern middle-aged faces of the senior officers, their heads already grizzled and grey; the intelligent, bright-eyed ones of the junior officers, trying to suppress their excitement and maintain their demeanour as naval officers; and the frankly exuberant, flushed faces of the midshipmen, sixteen and seventeen year-olds, thrilled beyond measure to be part of these great events. But they were the faces of men who were to be sacrificed to raise that common standard. They would live to see the first fruits of this bold mission off the coast of the New World, but only just: Churchill would achieve his aim of bringing the United States into the war on Britain's side. But then they would die, all of them – *violently* – on the other side of the world. All of them, sad and serious, lecher and innocent, young and old, were at that moment of triumph already doomed men…

BOOK FOUR

Escape to the Reich

'Ende gut, alles gut'

Old German saying

CHAPTER 1

'Ten stocky U-boats in a ragged line, U-23 drops and stops out leaving us nine... Nine plucky U-boats ... U-50 is overtaken now we are eight... Eight sturdy U-boats–'

'Can we have an end to that mournful dirge, Frenssen?' Christian asked, as the U-69 ploughed steadily across the bay after having dropped its fake wreckage, including poor Hinrichs's body, near the northern outlet. 'It is not exactly apt at this particular moment, is it?'

'But it's true, sir, ain't it?' Frenssen maintained doggedly. 'There's only one of us left, sir – and I did make it up mesen. I'm a po-et and didn't know it.' He grinned mightily at the Skipper.

'I know what you are, you big rogue, but I'd better keep that piece of particularly nasty information to myself.' He forgot Frenssen and concentrated on his instruments. By now they had almost completed their dog-leg back and forth across the inland water. Soon it would be night and they would be able to surface and save their electric motors. Before them lay an opening of some ninety kilometres in breadth. The

235

question was: where would they cross it? He turned to the two hydrophone operators. 'Anything?' he asked.

Von Arco, unshaven and unwashed, slumped on the floor untidily, roused himself from his stupor and followed the direction of Christian's look, his eyes dull and emotionless now, as if he had spent all his fear and could feel nothing any more.

The two of them eased their earphones slightly and replied, 'Nothing, sir.'

Christian nodded. It was a good sign. It looked indeed as if they had shaken off their pursuers – for the time being. Now he knew that if he could get out of the damned bay and into the Atlantic, he could bring the U-69 home. He'd take her away from the main Allied shipping routes, right up to the Arctic Circle, where there would be no convoys and no escort vessels. The weather would be damnable, of course, but that didn't matter; there, at least, he would not be confronted by destroyers and Allied aircraft. He looked at his watch. It was nearly nine o'clock. In these regions at this time of the year it would be almost dark. He made his decision. He'd take her up. 'Take her up to periscope height, please,' he ordered.

The motor hummed and stopped. Christian swung poor old Grizzly Bear's battered white cap from back to front. As skipper he was the only one on board who wore a white cap; the rest wore dark-blue. He bent and there was the gentle click of switches as he raised the gleaming steel tube. As always the crew stared at him expectantly, for he was their only link with the outside world.

Christian switched on low power and began to turn the periscope slowly across the darkened horizon then stopped abruptly, gasping with shock, as if someone had just slid a knife into his stomach.

'What is it?' von Arco hissed.

For a moment, Christian simply could not reply, as his petrified gaze took in what lay to the U-69's immediate front. It was too unbelievable for words.

'Jungblut,' von Arco said urgently, 'what in three devils' name *is it?*'

Suddenly Christian did not know whether he should curse or shout with joy, as he stared out at that magnificent panorama. 'What is it?' he echoed, as the crew stared at him open-mouthed like a bunch of village yokels. 'I'll tell you. Only about half the American fleet, plus...'

'Well, go on, sir,' Frenssen urged. 'Don't hang us by the dong!'

'Plus – well come and look for yourself, Frenssen.'

The burly petty officer didn't need a second invitation. He strode forward, shoving his little side hat to the edge of his cropped skull, and peered through the tube.

'Holy strawsack!' he gasped. There at anchor lay row after row of beautiful white ships like those he remembered from peacetime regattas at Kiel. But it was not the American ships riding calmly at anchor which caught Frenssen's attention. It was the great grey camouflaged shape of the battleship which was anchored in their centre, with the limp red and white flag hanging from its stern.

'Do you see it, *Obermaat?*' Christian asked.

'*And how!* I've got my glassy orbits on it this very minute, sir,' Frenssen hissed, turning the handles to high power. 'It's the frigging *Prince of Wales!* I recognise it from the identification charts!'

'Yes, the frigging *Prince of Wales* it is,' Christian agreed and, turning to the awe-struck crew, added, 'Yes, comrades, it's true, it's the one that carried Churchill across the Atlantic … the one we were after all the time.' He paused suddenly, face abruptly sombre, as he remembered all the others who had died in vain – Thorn, Hartmann, Kammhuber – in their attempt to sink the great ship.

Von Arco watched the change in Christian's expression and caught his breath. He stared up at the other officer and asked in a small voice, 'You're not going to attempt anything, are you, Jungblut…? Please, tell me!' His fear was all too evident.

Christian did not answer immediately. He could do it, he knew that. The great fleet up top was not operational. Neither their radar nor asdic was working. It would be as easy as falling off a log. He could slam his tin fish into the *Prince of Wales* and be off before the Tommies realized what had happened to them. It would be the sinking of the *Royal Oak* back in '39 all over again.

For a few moments he considered, his sombre look changing to one of quiet, sardonic amusement, while everyone stared at him in the sudden silence, wondering what was going through his head. With one simple order, Christian told himself, he could kill Churchill and perhaps change the whole course of 20th century history. It was a tempting possibility, even if he and the crew of the U-69 all died in the process. Immortal, albeit dead, at the ripe old age of twenty-three!

Slowly he shook his head. 'No, we will not kill Mr Churchill – *this time*,' he chuckled softly. 'Let the old man live. Now my sole concern is to get you bunch of rogues back alive to the Homeland.' He looked around the circle of their pale faces. 'Too many good men have died already.' He raised his voice and turned to Frenssen, still glued to the periscope. 'All right, *Obermaat*, down periscope,' he ordered a little wearily. 'You've had your moment of hob-nobbing with the great. Now let's get out of this damned bay...'

Now the lone submarine, the last survivor of the wolf packs, fought her way steadily ever northwards, fighting the thundering gales that came straight from the Arctic Circle and the mountainous seas. Now life became an endless icy drudgery. Night after night of roaring, hurtling seas, cold scratch meals and always dampness, a cloying, clinging dampness that pervaded everything. Icy seawater poured down the conning tower as soon as they surfaced to recharge the batteries every night and sluiced the control room, spreading throughout the boat till it reached the bilges so that everyone was always soaked and damp. Trying to sleep enough to go on watch – two hours on, four off – was cruel torture. All the time Christian felt baggy-eyed and sleepy, hating with a passion that hand shaking him to say, 'You're on, sir. It's wet and cold up top again'; trying to slip back into the delightful warm cocoon of sunny beaches and lightly-clad blondes, and unable to do so because he knew *he* was the only one who was going to save these men snoring behind their swaying curtains in the damp chaos of the U-69. Then out once again into a night as black as the devil, the shrieking wind full of vicious icy spray, to spend yet another two hours of timeless misery, peering slit-eyed into the howling storm, ducking periodically as the water leapt up at him with seemingly deliberate malice.

240

Even when submerged, the handful of men alone out there in that forgotten edge of the world had little peace. The waves were so deep that at periscope depth the U-69 swung back and forth on a crazy pendulum. Controlling depth was highly difficult so that, in spite of the danger to their electric batteries, they were forced to drop to the comparative peace of the deep water in order to get some rest. In the end, Christian had to order von Arco to take his share of the watches, although he knew just how craven and unreliable the latter was and how much the crew hated taking orders from him; for he simply could not go on any longer as the only deck officer.

But as they drew ever closer to the Arctic Circle the winds began to moderate somewhat. The sky started to clear and at last they were able to check their position by observation instead of dead reckoning. At night the flaming backdrop of the Aurora Borealis flushed the stars green and purple and every day at noon the sun was noticeably lower in the southern sky. Gradually they began to recover from the effects of the stormy weather and dry their clothes out. For the first time the cook was able to prepare a real hot meal for them. They had pea soup, filled with great lumps of tinned beef: *'Green fart-water complete with dead men's toes!'* as Frenssen proclaimed it loudly; but despite his description he ate it as heartily as the rest did and demanded another portion when he had bolted his down.

Now, as time passed, they climbed the world's shoulder, crossing the Arctic Circle with the days growing steadily shorter and colder. They took a wide sweep round the northern tip of Norway and began heading south. Still Christian maintained radio silence. Although most of Norway was occupied by German troops, he did not want to attract the Russians on Kola Island.

It was about this time that Christian began to notice a change in von Arco. His bearing started to become more military and he was snappy with crew members who seemed to be too slow for him. His face took on some of that old arrogance and once Christian, staggering out of his bunk to go on watch topside, found him wearing the battered white cap that only a skipper wore in a submarine on active service. He had flushed and handed it over to a still sleepy Christian with some sort of mumbled excuse.

It was just above Bergen, the northern-most U-boat base of the *Kriegsmarine,* that von Arco first attempted to reassert his old authority. Dawn was about to break and they were ready to dive when he snapped in that old, biting, arrogant manner of his, 'I say *Leutnant* Jungblut, don't you think it is time to break radio silence now and ask permission to run into Bergen? In Murwik they must be crying out for news, eh?'

Slowly Christian turned to look at him in the pale silver light of the stars that specked the cold northern sky, noting how the craven look had vanished from his face and how the shoulders were squared again in that Prussian manner von Arco affected in imitation of the Big Lion. 'And what would you like to report to Murwik, *Kapitänleutnant* von Arco?' He emphasized the other man's rank contemptuously. 'How you were fool enough to allow seven good boats and their crews to go to the bottom of Placentia Bay, perhaps? Or how you have proved to every man on the U-69 just what a damn coward you are, with a yellow streak a metre wide down the small of your back?' Christian's eyes blazed with sudden anger, as he realized for the first time that if and when they finally reached the Homeland, there would have to be a reckoning with von Arco; and it would be his word against that of a superior officer. 'No, *Herr Kapitänleutnant,* we will *not* request permission to run into Bergen and chance the Tommies picking up our signal so they'll have a nice big fat Hudson waiting for us off the harbour. No, *Herr Kapitänleutnant* von Arco, we shall maintain radio silence,' he rasped, voice harsh and biting, 'until *I*, the Skipper, decide to break it. Is that understood?' He glared so belligerently at the other man that von Arco moved back hastily, as if he were afraid that Christian might strike him.

'But I was only trying–' von Arco quavered.

'Is that understood?' Christian interrupted him brutally.

'Yes, I understand,' von Arco answered, lowering his eyes to hide the look of murder in them.

'Good, then get below and prepare the boat to dive.'

'Yessir,' von Arco mumbled and went below, his face contorted with hate, his mind seething. Behind him, Christian stared at the vast purple sweep of the northern sky, realizing for the first time that they were almost home, but realizing, too, there would be trouble ahead. How much trouble he could not, at that moment, possibly visualize…

CHAPTER 2

The days passed uneventfully as they plodded down the coast of Norway, keeping within sight of land but away from the coastal shipping routes; for Christian was taking no chances that they might be spotted by some seemingly harmless Norwegian fishing boat in the pay of the English.

The land had a brooding stillness about it, more of sullenness perhaps, Christian could not help thinking. It was all black cliff or white mountain peak. Occasionally, although it was still summer, blinding snowstorms came sweeping off the land without warning and were gone as quickly; those on duty on deck would come off watch beating the snow from their leather suits, their faces pinched and purple with the bitter cold.

The evenings were the best part of the day for the men of the U-69. After the only really hot meal of the day, those off duty were allowed for the first time to light up their cigarettes or pipes, for the hatch above was open and fresh air was streaming in, driving away the fetid stink of oil and sweat. They would sit in the crowded chaos in the glowing red light of the swinging lamps, talking of God and the world until finally someone would yawn and say: '*Na ja, genug für heute* – I'm gonna hit the hay!' Slowly they would drift to their tight bunks while Christian would go up on the bridge to have a last check before sleeping himself, breathing in the cold salty air and urinating in the 'pig's ear' as they called the hole specially designed for that purpose. Then it would be down below again, glad that another day had passed without problems, another day bringing them closer to home and safety...

Three weeks after they had finally escaped from Placentia Bay, they began to enter the narrows between Norway and Denmark, spending more time on the surface now that they had almost reached the security of German-dominated waters. Yet all the same, Christian did not relax his guard one bit. How many other U-boat skippers had been caught out here, just because they had felt *now* they could relax! Here the Royal Navy and the RAF were at their most active, knowing how easy it was to pin-point a target in this narrow strip of water that led into the Baltic.

Von Arco, for his part, had become increasingly insistent that Christian should break radio silence and contact U-boat HQ at Murwik. Once, in exasperation, Christian had cried at him, 'Goddammit to hell, von Arco, will you hold your trap! Or *I'll kick you off the damned bridge!'*

But von Arco had not reacted in that usual craven manner of his. Instead he had said, unimpressed by the threat, 'Do remember who you are talking to, Jungblut. After all, I *am* your superior officer even if you are the skipper of this stinking old tube!'

Christian had been so exasperated that he had been unable to reply, though Frenssen, who had watched the exchange, growled later, 'You should have kicked that arse-with-ears overboard, sir – that's what the shitehawk deserves before he can make any more frigging trouble!' Later Christian realized that the big *Obermaat* had been right, but by then it was too late...

On the 1st September 1941, Christian ordered radio silence to be broken at last. He called the radioman up to the bridge and dictated a brief signal to him to be sent to Admiral Doenitz, the Big Lion himself. In it he reported his position, what had happened over the last weeks and ended it with a request: 'Deem it proper that the U-69 should be guided into the safety of home waters by an escort vessel.' He knew the request was unusual. At that stage of the U-boat war, with the RAF and the Royal Navy not as active in German coastal waters as they would be later, it was not customary to send out an escort for a returning submarine. But Christian was taking no chances now, after such a long and hazardous voyage half-way across the world, of being caught out by a Tommy seaplane or running foul of a new minefield laid since they had last left port. He wanted some minesweeper or coastal trawler to guide him in and ensure that the risks were minimized. As he growled to Frenssen, 'We've taken risks enough, let some of those goddam base stallions at Kiel or Emden stick their necks out for a change.'

'Quite right too, sir,' Frenssen agreed heartily, 'we've been up to our hooters in shit on the poor old U-69 long enough. Let the old boat sail in in style. Yessir!'

But there would be no sailing in 'in style' for the U-69. Her days were numbered. Now she had only hours more to live...

It was just after dark that von Arco took over the watch. Some of the instruments down below were beginning to act up, as was often the case towards the end of a long patrol, and Christian busied himself supervising their adjustment, leaving von Arco above. He reasoned that now their voyage was almost over, von Arco could do little damage. All he had to do was report the approach of their guide. So he applied himself to the task on hand, his mind half-occupied by thoughts of a bath, a shave and the pleasures of the town to come. My God, he hadn't had a woman for nearly two months now!

Frenssen's mind seemed to be occupied by the same subject, for as he handed the sweating mechanics their tools and at the same time checked that nothing was left behind in the machinery once it had been adjusted, he moaned to no one in particular, 'You know, mates, I've got so much frigging ink in my fountain pen, I don't know who to frigging write to first! Great balls of flying crap, those pavement pounders back in the *Reeperbahn* better be ready and waiting for me when I get back, cos...' He shook his head as if almost overcome by emotion. ''Cos when I get off this tub *I'll have a blue-veiner on me that yer could cut frigging diamonds with!*'

Alone on the bridge save for the deck lookout, von Arco had other thoughts on his mind, now that they were almost home. He knew now that that cocky young swine Jungblut would blab. Even if he didn't, the crew would and the rumours of his conduct back at Placentia Bay would finally reach the ears of the Big Lion. And he knew the Admiral. He was a stickler for discipline. He would demand a court martial and that would be the end of his career and his dreams of becoming an admiral. The mission had been a failure, of course, too. But that wouldn't be so bad if he could only keep the matter of his conduct dark. The U-69 had survived and fought its way home against all odds, hadn't it? He frowned into the velvet night, the sky overhead pocked here and there by the faint silver glow of a star. What in three devils' name was he going to do? How was he going to save himself from the disgrace that would inevitably descend upon him once they reached land?

Time passed leadenly on the bridge as they ploughed steadily eastwards towards the Baltic and home. 'Should I go forrard, sir?' the deck lookout cut into his brooding, 'and see if I can see her. She can't be far off now, sir.'

'Yes,' von Arco answered moodily. 'Do as you wish.' The lookout muttered something under his breath and clattered down the ladder to post himself at the bows. 'Rebellious swine!' von Arco grunted. They were all alike, this pack of the U-69. God, how he wished he had never laid eyes on the bunch of mutinous swine!

Suddenly his mind was wrenched from his own problems by the call from the bows, 'Trawler ahead, sir... Must be our escort!'

Von Arco flung up his binoculars and gasped. If this was their escort it was dangerously close and seemingly still unaware of the presence of the U-69. Goddammit, he'd have to switch on the lights so that she could see the submarine, wallowing there low down in the water. He was just about to call out to the deck lookout to do so, when the plan came to him, prepared, complete, total. *It was the way out!*

'Full astern together!' he yelled into the voice tube.

'Sir, she's not seen us!' the deck lookout cried furiously as the U-69 suddenly surged forward. *'She's gonna hit—'*

His words ended in a shrill scream of absolute agony as the trawler slammed into the U-69 with a great booming echo of metal striking metal.

For one long moment the two craft stayed there, locked together by the impetus of the trawler's headway, the only sound the thunder of the latter's engines and the shrieks of the dying lookout whose legs had been severed by the impact. Suddenly, with a sickening rending of metal, the trawler tore herself free. Von Arco, his face contorted in a look of frenzied, diabolic triumph, hesitated no longer. He ripped off his heavy sea-boots and prepared for what had to come.

It did. As the lights started to blaze on the trawler and angry voices began to break the silence of the night, he clambered down the side of the conning tower in his stockinged feet, already noting the rapidly increasing list of the stricken submarine.

'We've hit a sub!' someone yelled frantically on the trawler. 'Turn that frigging searchlight to frigging port, willya!' For one moment he allowed himself to be illuminated by that icy white beam now cutting the velvet darkness and then, with the same ease that had once made him the *Kriegsmarine's* pre-war diving champion, he sliced neatly into the grey water of the North Sea.

Just in time. Behind him the U-69 gave a sickening lurch. She heeled alarmingly, her conning tower almost touching the surface of the sea before she righted herself. But the damage had already been done.

'Heaven, arse and cloudburst!' someone on the now stationary trawler cried out in shocked alarm. 'She's going down... *She's frigging well going down!*'

The finger of bright white light ran the length of the stricken submarine. She was indeed going down. The water was bubbling in white, frothy and furious through the great jagged gap in her midships; tons of it.

Von Arco paused in his swimming, tossing his head to one side to avoid the low swell so that he could get a better look at the sinking submarine. He was safe, he knew that. At intervals the searchlight slipped over in his direction and there were already dark figures poised with landing nets at the bows waiting to pull him aboard. In spite of the icy cold, he felt a warm glow of success surge through his body. He had done it after all. *He had done it! He was free of them at last!*

With dramatic suddenness it happened. There was a muffled *crump!* as the ammunition locker on the U-69 exploded. Crouched in the water as he was, von Arco gasped with shock, as if someone had just punched him in the guts. The doomed submarine's stern rose into the sky, her screws churning purposelessly, like a great steel tomb. For a moment she remained thus. Then, slowly, inexorably, she started to slide beneath the waves. They leapt up greedily to consume her, only to recoil, hissing and spluttering angrily, as they felt the searing heat of her boilers. But there was no staying them. With one last wild tumult of boiling white water, the U-69 was gone for good.

Moments later helping hands were dragging von Arco out of the sea, his heart wild with triumph…

CHAPTER 3

'There will have to be an inquiry, you realize, von Arco,' Admiral Doenitz said, though the usual sternness had vanished from his voice as he gazed at the younger officer's bedraggled figure. Von Arco was still clad in the rough hand-me-downs they had found for the lone survivor of the U-69 on board the trawler. For shocked as he was, he had insisted on being sent to Murwik to report immediately. Now he no longer presented the elegant figure of a staff officer that he had when Doenitz had seen him off on the start of his bold mission.

'Of course, it will be a mere formality,' Doenitz continued, gazing out at the grey September morning and the new recruits for the U-boat arm, training down below on the parade ground. 'The blame for the collision clearly lies with the skipper of the trawler. He should have known that ships meeting in a channel should pass *port to port*. I have already suspended him from his command and placed him under open arrest here.'

Von Arco breathed an inner sigh of relief. 'Under those conditions out there, sir, last night, it could have happened to anyone,' he said magnanimously.

'You are a generous man, a very generous man, von Arco, after what you have been through. I know it well. I suffered the same fate back in 1918 and that was in the Med, where the water is considerably warmer than in the North Sea.'

'Any hope for them?' Von Arco lowered his voice, his face showing apparent concern. 'I mean for the chaps of the U–' He broke off, as if he could not contain his emotions any longer.

Admiral Doenitz shook his head. 'I doubt it. We've already got rescue craft out there, of course, and the wreck has been very accurately plotted. That was one thing the trawler skipper did right. We're sending out divers from Kiel at,' he consulted the elegant silver watch the Führer himself had given him, 'just about now. But I think they'll have little success. Bad weather is forecast for the North Sea later in the day and those damned Tommy Hudsons are active again.' He cleared his throat noisily and forced a smile. 'All right, von Arco, first have a rest. I shall expect your full report on the sinking, and a tentative one on Operation Death Watch, on my desk by zero eight hundred hours tomorrow morning. I shall convene the court of inquiry for fourteen hundred hours the same day. That is all, von Arco.'

Von Arco clicked to attention in his old

style and barked, as if he were on parade, 'I shall clean up, sir, and commence the reports at once. You will have them on your desk by zero eight hundred tomorrow, *sir!*'

Doenitz's hard face relaxed for a moment and he said, his voice as warm as it could ever be, 'Thank you, von Arco. You are a man after my own heart. I predict a great future for you in the *Kriegsmarine.*'

'Thank you, sir!'

'*Morgen,* von Arco.'

'*Morgen, Herr Admiral!*'

With that Doenitz bent his cropped head back to his papers and plans, leaving von Arco to walk out in a joyful daze. In spite of his tiredness, his mind buzzed. This exceeded his wildest dreams. A culprit for the disaster had already been found and there were no survivors. He was in the clear; the U-69 had vanished for good, taking her secrets with her. At that moment, von Arco could have kissed even the square-headed drill instructor yelling at the red-faced recruits as they hopped gasping across the parade ground, rifles extended full-length. *It was going to be all right!*

It was Frenssen who had reacted first – and correctly – as the U-69 received that tremendous, savage blow which flung Christian from his feet. He had let his spanner drop, as if red-hot, crying fervently in the same instant, 'Shut the water-tight doors… Shut them for Chrissake, *we've been hit!*'

Thereafter things had happened fast. A violent crash came from the torpedo-storage room, followed by the startlingly blue and red flare-up of an electrical explosion. Almost immediately the ammunition for the deck gun had begun to detonate. Now the U-69 was going down at a crazy angle, reeling from port to starboard, throwing men and gear into confusion, a jumbled mess of arms and legs.

The lights went out. Men screamed hysterically. Now they could feel the water surging in everywhere. Somehow Christian struggled to his feet. The water was pouring into the control compartment, as the boat listed at twenty degrees. Together with Frenssen, who was cursing furiously, they managed to shut their own water-tight door so that the control room was sealed off from the rest of the dying boat.

At last Christian managed to shake off the paralysing shock of that terrible impact and began to take stock of their situation, as Frenssen found a torch somewhere and switched it on to reveal that there were four of them in the control room: Jungblut, Frenssen, Frahm and a leading hand, a fitter, who had been repairing the defective instruments when they had been struck.

'Let's have some more light, *Obermaat,*' he

ordered, trying to keep calm in spite of the fact that his brain was pounding. 'There should be some more hand-lamps over there. But give me your torch first.'

Frenssen handed him the light and he splashed off to find the hand-lamps. He flashed a beam on the depth gauges. To his surprise he found that they were both reading little over twenty metres. They had not gone down as deeply as he had thought. As Frenssen and the leading hand, a big, burly blond fellow named Schmitz, flicked on the hand-lamps and the water-logged compartment flooded with yellow light, Christian said: 'I don't think we can *blow* her up. We've taken too much water and we had full buoyancy when we were hit.' The other three absorbed the information while the seawater continued to pour in relentlessly, reminding them that their time was limited. All about them the electric contacts spat venomously in a flurry of angry blue sparks, as the water rose and shorted them.

'What's the drill, sir, then?' Frenssen asked meekly, his usual boldness vanished. Now there was something pathetic, almost humble about the huge man. Like the rest, he stared at Christian's pale face expectantly, like a child staring at a wise mother who always knew how to solve life's problems.

Christian swallowed his angry retort and told himself to be calm, trying to shrug off

258

the mental concussion of the sinking. 'Well, Frenssen, I think we've got to help ourselves, quite frankly. I am sure they will have marked our position up top. But before they can get specialized lifting and rescue gear out here...' He stopped and pointed the torch at the bubbling green water which had now reached well beyond his ankles, making his point without words.

'Christ on a crutch!' Schmitz quavered. 'And I can't even friggingly well swim!'

That made them laugh and the tension relaxed a little, as Christian racked his brain for a way out, splashing around the tight, littered compartment as he did so until finally he found himself directly under the conning tower. 'Well,' he said finally, 'I suppose we can climb up there. At least it'll get us out of this bloody freezing water.'

One minute later Frenssen, on top of the tight ladder leading upwards, made his discovery. 'Sir,' he cried, peering through the port of the upper window, the glass of which had withstood the terrific pressure, *there's light outside!* I can see it!'

'You can?' Christian asked excitedly.

'Definite!'

'That means there is somebody up there. It must be a searchlight or something. Frahm, what do you think the height of this conning tower is?'

'I know it exactly, sir,' the engineer

replied. 'It's five metres fifty.'

'So that means the top of the hatch is about fifteen metres from the surface – about, say, the height of eight men standing on top of each other.'

'Something like that,' Frahm agreed. 'But what are you hinting at, sir?'

'This: if we can get out of the boat, we should be able to swim to the surface, even without rescue apparatus, and be picked up.'

The leading hand Schmitz moaned, but this time his concern was genuine. 'I feel I'm gonna puke, sir,' he said miserably.

'Then frigging well spill yer cookies, it'll shut your trap!' Frenssen said unsympathetically. 'Can't frigging well hear mesen think for all yer frigging chat!'

'I'm going to shut the lower hatch,' Christian went on. 'With a bit of luck, we might get a bubble of trapped air to rush us to the surface.'

He grunted and turned the clips so that now four of them balanced on the ladder, each man's face virtually buried in the rump of the next. 'Like frigging sardines in a frigging can!' as Frenssen snorted indignantly, '*without the frigging oil!*'

'Now the drill is simple,' Christian continued, trying to keep his voice calm and reasonable. 'We open the hatch above and let in the sea. As it comes in, each man will fill his lungs with as much air as he can and climb out double-quick time.'

'But I can't swim,' the leading hand began miserably and, retching suddenly, was sick all over Frenssen's head.

'Oh my fucking Christ!' Frenssen yelled. 'Not only do they frigging well trap me at the bottom of the frigging sea, but they puke on me as well. *What a frigging life!*'

'What a frigging life, indeed!' Christian echoed and then snapped curtly, 'All right, Frahm, see if you can open the top hatch!'

The engineer officer, who was at the top of the ladder now, bent his shoulder against the hatch awkwardly and heaved with all his strength. Nothing happened! The hatch cover remained firmly in place.

'Give it some more grunt!' Christian urged.

Frahm tried again, his face purple in the yellow light of the torch, sweat dripping down his furrowed brow. 'Sorry,' he gasped. 'Can't open the whoreson!'

Christian thought for a moment, then he had it. While they had been trying to open the hatch, the pressure in the control room below them must have been building up. He bent awkwardly and opened the clips. Sure enough there came the sharp hiss of air forcing its way into the tower. 'How about that?' he cried happily. 'Try it now!'

'Watch it, sir!' Frenssen yelled, wiping the vomit from his face and trying at the same time to support Schmitz who had now lapsed into a semi-conscious state. 'I think I can smell chlorine gas.'

'You're right,' Christian said urgently. 'The water's got to the batteries! Come on, Frahm. Move it!'

The engineer 'moved' it, knowing that they now ran the risk of choking to death in the deadly battery gas. Coughing and spluttering, his eyes already beginning to run in the acrid fumes, he exerted his full weight and heaved.

'*Los ... los....!*' Christian urged, choking on the gas, the tears streaming down his contorted face, ready to close the bottom hatch as soon as the clips turned.

'Here they come,' Frahm choked. 'They're moving... She's gonna open, the son ... of ... a ... *bitch!*'

Christian hesitated no longer as the upper hatch started to creak open. He bent hurriedly, blinded by tears, choking and coughing like some ancient asthmatic in the throes of an attack, and closed the bottom hatch, feeling the first trickle of water from above descending upon his bent shoulders. 'All right, comrades, now take your time. Do you hear me, Schmitz?'

'Yessir,' the leading hand said weakly, shaking his head like a man trying to rouse himself from a deep sleep.

'We're going to do this. Strip off to your

underclothes, and get rid of yer boots.'

'That's the stuff to give the troops,' Frenssen said gleefully. 'Fourteen days' survivors leave for this. By the Great God and All His Triangles, I'll be stripping a few mattress-pounders during it, believe you me!' He started to pull off his boots.

Christian grinned, grateful yet again for the big petty officer's coarse humour. Frenssen certainly knew how to defuse a tense situation. 'All right then, everybody ready?'

'*Ready ... ready ... ready!*' came back the cries of the others, shivering now in their underclothes.

'*Gut.* Frahm, open the hatch– *FULL!*'

Christian tensed and then it happened. The sea crashed in and everything went black...

CHAPTER 4

'This court of inquiry is now convened,' Admiral Doenitz snapped and, unbuckling his sword, laid it formally in front of him on the big desk and sat down. On either side of him the two senior captains prepared to hear the evidence.

Swiftly the clerk to the court of inquiry read out the facts pertaining to the sinking of the U-69 and then called, 'Lieutenant Brandmeyer!'

In spite of his junior rank, Lieutenant Brandmeyer, a burly, red-faced man who had the look of a professional seaman about him, turned out to be almost as old as Admiral Doenitz himself. He rolled forward, obviously awkward in his best dress blues, clutching his dirk as if he badly needed its reassurance.

The clerk wasted no time. *'Leutnant zur See* Brandmeyer, will you please explain how this unfortunate accident came about?' he said briskly and it was clear from his voice that he felt it was all Brandmeyer's fault.

The old officer flushed. Sitting on a chair near the wall von Arco smirked to himself. The man was as guilty as hell. Doenitz would roast him; he could see it from the icy look on the Big Lion's face. From now onwards it was going to be a matter of mere formality. Already that morning Doenitz had received his initial report on the failure of Operation Death Watch with a cold smile and the reassurance that, 'No blame can be attached to your conduct of the operation, von Arco. That wretched *Abwehr* fellow, Dr Ritter or whatever his damned name was, must have given away all the details of the operation to the English. Perhaps he had been in their pay all along. You know what a treacherous people the English are... Naturally you will be returning to my staff after you have had your survivors' leave.' Von Arco had been about to protest he did not need the leave, but then he had thought better of it and had shut his mouth.

In an awkward, hesitant fashion, the trawler Skipper recounted how he had seen the U-69 when it was too late, larding his account with plenty of local dialect words as if he did not feel too much at ease using High German. At the desk, Admiral Doenitz's frown deepened and von Arco told himself that the unfortunate Skipper was in for a lot of trouble. Doenitz regarded the U-boat arm almost as if it were a personal fleet. Anyone sinking one of his U-boats was really for the high jump. In the end the trawler Skipper simply dried up and the clerk of the court had to demand sharply, 'Well, Lieutenant, is that all?'

Numbly the latter indicated it was and was ordered to sit down, while the two senior captains made hurried notes on the pads in front of them.

'*Kapitänleutnant* von Arco, please come to the stand now,' the clerk ordered.

Elegant in his best uniform, the Knight's Cross glittering at his throat, von Arco stepped forward gripping his dress sword and made a small bow to the bench. Swiftly the clerk went through the formalities and then said: 'Please, *Herr Kapitänleutnant,* will you now give us your account of what happened last night.' And by the look on the clerk's moonlike, bespectacled face, von Arco could see whose side he was on – *his*. The clerk knew which side his bread was buttered. Von Arco was Doenitz's man and the clerk wanted to be on the winning team.

Von Arco cleared his throat and began his account confidently. 'On the night in question, I was in command of the U-69. We had had a long and dangerous voyage half-way across the world and I was allowing the crew to relax a little, confident now that we were safely home. All we needed was the patrol boat which my subordinate, the late Lieutenant Jungblut, had radioed for. Against my wishes, I might add. With all due modesty, I may say I was quite capable of taking the U-69 into...' Von Arco faltered and his words trailed away.

The court was not listening to him! He could see that in their eyes. Their expressions changed, from attentive listening to surprised shock. Even Doenitz's hatchet face registered astonishment. Slowly, very slowly, feeling now the draught from the open door behind him, von Arco began to turn. 'Oh, my God,' he blurted out, unable to restrain himself, face abruptly ashen with fear, 'It's ... *you*...!'

Like three grey ghosts they stood there, Christian, Frenssen and Frahm, their eyes filled with hate and accusation...

Christian had taken one last breath as the sea had engulfed him, the roaring filling his ears, knowing that there was nothing for it but to fight for life with all of man's primitive instincts for survival. Fighting the weight of water, he hauled himself up the ladder rung by rung. His head bumped into the leading hand's rump. With a strength born of despair, he pushed the reluctant sailor. His heel struck Christian's contorted face and then he was through the hatch, striving desperately to reach the surface.

Christian pushed upwards, his lungs threatening to burst at any moment, that great roaring in his ears, black and red stars exploding in front of his eyes. He struck out with quick, jerky breast-strokes, face upturned towards that faint yellow light which seemed impossibly far away. *God, would he ever make it!*

And then suddenly he was above the surface, coughing, spluttering, gasping in great draughts of the sweet night air and drinking in the blessed sight of the stars shining in that great velvet immensity of space.

For what seemed an age he simply trod water there, hardly able to believe his own tremendous good fortune, that he had survived, and then he heard the voices calling him. It was Frahm and Frenssen some fifty metres away, with beyond them two boats, one of them sweeping the surface with a searchlight. He took another breath and struck out to them, calling as he got closer, 'Where's Schmitz?'

'Had it, sir,' Frenssen replied and wiped the foam from his face. He reached under and pulled something up by the hair. It was the dead leading hand. 'Poor shiteheel. Why didn't he learn to swim?' He let Schmitz's head fall again.

'Thanks, Frenssen,' Christian said quietly. 'All right, stick together. Let's swim to that one with the searchlight.'

Five minutes later, the three of them were wrapped in blankets, drinking strong black tea laced with *Kümmel,* while the trawler's skipper told them what had happened and how the ship which had rammed the U-69 had sailed full speed for Emden to obtain rescue apparatus. All that night, they had hoped against hope that there would be other survivors from the U-69. But they had hoped in vain. Towards dawn an MTB carrying a diver had raced up. Hurriedly he had been sent down and had located the U-69 without too much difficulty. But as they had unscrewed his diving helmet he had shaken his head to a tense, anxious Christian and said softly, 'Not a hope, sir. I walked the whole length of hull, tapping with my spanner at every half a metre.' He had accepted gratefully the lit cigarette that someone thrust between his lips. He puffed then continued, 'There was not one reply... They must all have drowned almost immediately, sir.' He bent his head, as if in sudden shame.

'Thank you, diver,' Christian had replied and turned away.

A thin drizzle of gentle rain was now falling on the sea, but it did not depress him. He had lost his ship and his crew and knew he ought to be sad, but he wasn't really. Instead he was filled with an almost delirious joy at not being dead. Yet as the old battered trawler had begun to make its slow way back to Emden, that joy had gradually begun to turn to hatred for von Arco, who he now knew had sailed for land with the trawler which had rammed them, and a desire for revenge. Now that arrogant craven creature had become the focus for all his hurt, sorrow and rage. *Von Arco would have to pay!*

Now, as he confronted von Arco at last, Christian felt a strange sense of detached calm, almost as if he were a spectator at some melodrama which did not move him to any great extent; watching the events unfold in a cold, emotionless manner: the surprised look on the faces of the senior captains; the fat clerk's open-mouthed astonishment; von Arco's terrified ashen features and trembling hands; and the growing sternness on Doenitz's face, as if he already knew that von Arco was at fault and that he, the Big Lion, had been tricked.

'It is *Leutnant zur See* Jungblut, isn't it?' Doenitz's harsh incisive rasp broke the brooding silence of the court.

Christian clicked to attention, awkward in the borrowed gumboots. 'Yessir,' he snapped. 'Reporting with Engineer Officer Frahm and *Obermaat* Frenssen, the survivors of the crew of the U-69.'

Doenitz mustered them coldly, while von Arco stared at them in carven horror, as if they were ghosts from another world come back to haunt him, which in a way they were. 'Stand at ease,' Doenitz ordered and then said, 'And why have you entered this court of inquiry in such a manner, Lieutenant?'

'Because I feel I have something of the

greatest important to say to it, sir,' Christian heard himself say, his voice calm and completely under control.

'Concerning what?'

'The events of Operation Death Watch, sir; and my witnesses here,' he indicated the other two, 'will bear me out, as the rest of my crew would have if they'd survived.'

'*Your* crew?' Doenitz queried. 'I thought *Kapitänleutnant* von Arco was in command of the U-69.' He flashed the white-faced officer in a hard searching look.

'I have been in command of the U-69 ever since *Kapitänleutnant* Baer was killed in action. I took her out to Newfoundland and I brought her back. For most of the way back' – for a moment Christian's hatred and contempt broke through – '*Herr Kapitänleutnant* von Arco,' Christian's lips curled contemptuously, 'was nothing better than supercargo!'

Doenitz's thin hatchet face flushed angrily. 'Are you telling me, man,' he bellowed, 'that *Kapitänleutnant* von Arco is telling a lie when he claims he commanded the U-69 on its voyage back?'

Christian stood his ground, unimpressed by the Big Lion's anger. 'Yessir, and undoubtedly he has told the court many other lies, too,' he declared stoutly.

'Do you understand what you are saying, Jungblut?' Doenitz barked. 'You are accusing a senior officer–' He spluttered and could not go on.

Christian hesitated no longer. Feeling absolutely confident and sure of himself, he snapped, 'Sir, I accuse *Kapitänleutnant* von Arco of cowardice in the face of the enemy, grave dereliction of duty and an absolute and complete breakdown of moral courage and conduct in the presence of subordinate officers and men!' He looked coldly at von Arco, who cowered there a broken man, shoulders slumped in defeat. 'I contend, sir, that *Kapitänleutnant* von Arco is not fit to hold a commission in the U-boat arm. That is all, sir.' Christian stopped, noting that he was not even breathing hard.

Next to him Frenssen whispered out of the side of his mouth, 'That sonofabitch couldn't even run a third-class knocking shop without getting his dick in the wringer!' and then tensed for the storm to come.

But it didn't come. Instead Doenitz said very quietly, 'Do you other two back up the grave charges made against *Kapitänleutnant* von Arco?'

'Yessir!' Frahm and Frenssen snapped as one.

Doenitz pursed his lips and turned to look at von Arco. 'It's true, isn't it, von Arco?' he said softly, taking in the latter's ashen face and trembling hands. In the last five minutes von Arco seemed to have shrunk. Now his elegant blue uniform seemed much too big for him.

'Yessir,' von Arco whispered, his voice barely audible. 'It is true ... Jungblut commandeered the U-69 all along ... I just ... broke down completely ... I couldn't help it...' Two large tears began to trickle slowly down his wan face and at that moment Christian knew he could not hate von Arco any more. He was too pathetic now to hate; indeed, he felt the first stirrings of pity for the broken man.

Doenitz considered for a moment before saying, 'I think the court of inquiry should recess, gentlemen, until we have considered the new evidence offered by the survivors of the U-69.' He rose to his feet and the senior captains hurriedly did so too, as if they could not get out of the place quickly enough. Doenitz buckled on his sword. 'Jungblut and you two others will go on survivors' leave as speedily as it can be possibly arranged.'

They clicked to attention.

Doenitz acknowledged their salute by touching his hand to his braided cap before striding out of the room, followed by the captains and the clerk. Not one of them ventured a glance at the broken man standing there in the middle of the room, looking absurd now in his trappings of glory: the uniform, the sword, the Knight's Cross.

For a moment the three survivors remained behind, standing there also in silence, before, as if to some unspoken command, they left, leaving *Kapitänleutnant* von Arco alone in the rays of weak sunshine that came in through the tall windows...

One hour later the afternoon calm of the officers' quarters at Murwik's naval barracks was disturbed by the sharp dry crack of a single pistol shot. Admiral Doenitz looked up momentarily from his papers and said quite simply to his aide, 'He has taken the officers' way out. It is simpler that way...' Then he bent his head and continued his work. Operation Death Watch was completed at last.

ENVOI

'SEVENTH: Such a peace should enable all men to traverse the high seas and oceans without hindrance.'

Article Seven of the Atlantic Charter, published in Washington and London, and agreed at Placentia Bay, August 1941

Tiny men were jumping, panic-stricken into the sea from the high defence control towers as the great ship began to list alarmingly, thick black oily smoke pouring from her ruptured boilers. One man did a spectacular dive, the aerial camera of the low-flying Japanese dive-bomber catching the action perfectly. He knifed into the boiling sea far below, already littered with bomb-shattered debris and shouting, struggling men, and started swimming away from the dying ship. Another risked that awesome dive and failed. He slammed into the sloping deck and toppled over the side like a sack of wet cement.

The newsreel commentator was beside himself with excitement, as he rhapsodised about the next flight of Japanese dive-bombers coming in at mast-top height, zooming unscathed through the tremendous barrage put up by the trapped British ships, his voice hoarse and hysterical: *'Nothing can escape these brave, fanatical Japanese pilots who are Germany's newest allies in the great battle against the decadent Anglo-American pluto-crats... They die gladly for their beloved Emperor, with their well-known cry of triumph on their lips – BANZAI...!'*

The soundtrack took over again, full of the snarl of the diving planes, the whine of the bombs, the frenetic chatter of the machine-guns. Among that enthralled audience of civilians and servicemen in the station's newsreel cinema, packing it out to see the latest news from the front, a sickened *Kapitänleutnant* Christian Jungblut was glad of the respite. That gloating commentator's voice nauseated him; he wished he had not come inside to kill the last few minutes before his train arrived. How could anyone find pleasure in the death of such fine ships, even if they were enemy ones?

Now it was clear to Christian's expert eye that nothing could save the pride of the Royal Navy. The newsreel showed how one torpedo-bomber, with the rising sun marker on its sleek wings, came bursting through the smoke and flak-peppered sky at mast-height to launch its torpedo. It struck the water nose-heavy and immediately churned a thin white wake straight for that beautiful ship. The torpedo exploded with a great roar at her bows, sending her reeling into her death throes. There was a flash-shot to the inside of the plane's cockpit to reveal a sweat-glazed, fanatical yellow face crying, 'Banzai.' Immediately the commentator sprang into action once more: *'Thus the death blow is struck,'* he crowed triumphantly, *'not only to the pride of England's Navy, but to*

the whole of Mr Churchill's vaunted Empire.
Look how the English ship sinks!'

Suddenly there was silence. The Japanese cameras showed how the bow of the stricken battleship rose straight into the air like the steeple of an enormous steel cathedral. For one long moment they focused on the name written there and then, with startling abruptness as the audience rose to their feet shouting and clapping, yelling *'Sieg Heil'* over and over again, the great 35,000 ton *Prince of Wales* slid to the bottom of the Pacific and there was nothing there but the Japanese planes circling the boiling water like vultures.

Christian had had enough. Hurriedly he rose to his feet and started to push his way through the cheering crowd, pulling aside the thick blackout curtain, grateful for the cold winter air and an end to the shouting. So that was how it ended, he told himself, standing there for a moment, watching the snowflakes falling in slow showers; that was how it would end for all of them who fought their battles at sea.

'Would you like a nice time, sailor-boy?' the warm inviting voice cut into his reverie. 'I do something special for sailors, *Schatz.'*

He turned, startled. The whore was pretty in a brassy, blonde way with her imitation fur jacket and too-short skirt, as she stared invitingly at Christian in open-lipped, professional concupiscence.

'*Anything* you like,' she simpered, fluttering her eyelashes.

'Ay, and I bet yer mother blows a trombone, as well!' a coarse, well-remembered beery voice guffawed. 'Beat it, my little beaver!'

'Go and stick yer dong up yer own orifice!' the whore cried indignantly. '*And give yersen a cheap thrill!*' She stalked away and started soliciting a pimply-faced youth in the armoured corps a few metres away.

Obermaat Frenssen laughed a little wearily and said, as he heaved his pack up more comfortably onto his big shoulders, 'So much for us heroes, sir, eh?'

'Yes, so much for heroes,' Christian agreed, picking up his case and walking through the usual seething mass of servicemen wandering around in a semi-bemused, alcoholic state, watched by the hard-eyed 'chaindogs' who were posted at all exits to the big, echoing station like prison guards.

They fought their way to the train which would take them to the submarine docks, the sides of the locomotive painted with the same old tired slogan: '*Wheels Roll For Victory*'.

A draft of ill-looking teenagers in poorly-fitting naval uniforms got in their path. 'Get them frigging cardboard sailors out of the way, willya!' Frenssen yelled at the young petty officer in charge. 'Can't ya see they're stopping two heroes from getting back to their frigging ship? Move it, arse-with-ears!'

Hurriedly the red-faced petty officer moved his charges out of the way, and out of the side of his mouth, flooding Christian's face with beery breath, Frenssen whispered, 'Poor sods. Lower than a whale's arse, the lot of 'em. Cannon-fodder written all over their ugly mugs!'

'Yes, I suppose you're right, you big rogue,' Christian agreed morosely, unable to get the fate of that great ship out of his mind as they battled to board the train.

In front Frenssen elbowed his way down the packed corridor heading for the emptier first class compartments although, as a chief petty officer, he was entitled only to second-class travel. He opened the door of the first carriage and cried, 'Room for a couple of heroes in here, comrade?'

The fat quartermaster-lieutenant looked up from his book and opened his mouth to protest, but changed his mind when he saw Christian with his three gold rings and Knight's Cross dangling from his throat. '*Guten Tag, die Herren,*' he said formally and looked down at his book hastily again, as Frenssen lifted his right leg and broke wind mightily before commenting, 'Good to get all that green smoke off my chest. Must have been something I ate.' He slumped into his seat and pulled out one of the half a dozen 'flatmen' he had concealed about his person.

'Did you have a good leave, you big rogue?' Christian asked.

Frenssen took a mighty slug, while the quartermaster peered at him over the edge of his book as if this great hulking man, his chest ablaze with medals and decorations, was a creature from another world, which in a way he was. 'Good leave? You betcha, sir! I bounced more mattress polkas than I had good dinners. At it till my back collar stud popped out!' He took another drink and stowed the flat bottle away reverently. Now that they were going on patrol again, those illicit flatmen were going to be more valuable than gold to him. 'All the same, sir, I'm glad to be going back to sea agen.'

'Glad?' Christian queried, looking at the darkening sky and the snowflakes still drifting down, his mood as sombre as this winter day.

'Why yes, sir, I mean they're only whores, you know. Professional gash. What other kind of gash would have anything to do with *heroes*' – he emphasized the word cynically – 'like us? They all know that the men of the U-boat command'll be for the chop sooner or later. So they want to get hitched to some feather merchant – a base stallion with a nice soft, safe job and a pension coming at the end of the war when our Führer has finally achieved final victory.' Frenssen looked sourly at the fat quartermaster, as if challenging him to object, then lapsed into a sullen silence.

The other man buried his head even deeper in his book. These front swine were a coarse, unpredictable lot, he told himself nervously; there should be some way of segregating them from decent, law-abiding people.

Silently, reading the quartermaster's look, Christian agreed. The front swine were another race from the base stallions. They really ought to be segregated...

Oberleutnant zur See Frahm, the U-44's executive, saluted smartly and snapped, breath fogging on the cold evening air, 'All hands on board, sir.'

Christian returned the salute and then clasped his old friend's hand warmly. 'Hello, old house. Weeds never die, I see!'

'Weeds never die!' Frahm echoed as Frenssen eyed the crew mustered on the casing behind the conning tower. There were fifty of them, all teenagers apart from a couple of petty officers whose chests bore the Iron Cross. 'Cardboard frigging sailors,' he muttered under his breath.

Christian waited till the roll-call was finished, unable to make out any of their faces in the grey gloom or recognize any of their names.

'All greenbeaks, sir,' Frahm commented

when it was over, 'except for the petty officers and the engineer officer,' then snapped, 'Crew now at harbour stations! Secured for sea!'

The new captain looked the length of his first command, the U-44, straight from the Blohm and Voss yard, and abruptly felt his mood of gloom vanish. 'Number One,' he barked in a fair imitation of old Grizzly Bear, dead these six months, 'stand the men at ease. I'll say a few words to them.'

Now Christian could hardly see their faces as he mounted the conning tower, smelling the boat's newness and knowing that soon it would be replaced by that familiar old stink of oil, sweat and human fear. 'Comrades, shipmates,' he began, addressing those grey ghosts standing below him, 'when we finally sail with the wolf packs, as we soon will, each and every one of you must carry this conviction in your heart that every enemy ship you encounter must be destroyed ruthlessly and without compassion! This winter, comrades, we must finally destroy the might of the Anglo-Americans once and for all. *Kameraden der U-Boot Waffe–*'

Distinctly Christian heard Frenssen's gasp of surprise and he stopped, horror-struck, suddenly aware of what he was saying and realizing who he was echoing. It was the same speech that Doenitz had given at Murwik the day that the men of the wolf packs had sailed to their deaths in the North Atlantic: harsh, brutal and unfeeling.

Abruptly Christian Jungblut was aghast at himself. He told himself he must never become like that. Glory was not everything. The lives of these raw, callow young men entrusted to his keeping were more important than all the glittering prizes and decorations in the world. 'Comrades,' he said, his voice no longer harsh and rasping, but soft and feeling, 'we have our duty to the Fatherland to perform, I know that and I think you do too, otherwise you would not have volunteered for the U-boat arm. But I would like you *always* to bear this in mind. It is not important to die for our beloved Germany.' He paused and stared down at those pale blurs, those thin blue shapes below, as if seeing the ghosts of all those who had gone before them, before saying simply, *'No, it is important to live for our country!* Thank you...'

'Three cheers for the Skipper,' Frenssen yelled, new hope in his voice, *'hip ... hip...'* But Christian had already disappeared below.

Five minutes later the U-44 was nosing its way down the snow-enshrouded Elbe, its bow pointed to the open sea and the new battles to come. Christian Jungblut was going to the wars again...

The publishers hope that this book has given you enjoyable reading. Large Print Books are especially designed to be as easy to see and hold as possible. If you wish a complete list of our books please ask at your local library or write directly to:

Dales Large Print Books
Magna House, Long Preston,
Skipton, North Yorkshire.
BD23 4ND